Albert Walk
A Collection of Short Stories
Andy Halpin

Contents.

The Birthday Wish

Lesley Bannister, an attractive brunette in her late twenties stepped off the train at the far end of the station and made her way along the platform with the rest of the crowd of day trippers that had been disgorged from the train and headed towards the row of barriers at the exit to the station and after retrieving her ticket from her multi coloured shoulder bag she proceeded to scan it at the electronic barriers and stepped out into the warm sunshine of Bray.

She stood for a moment at the exit as the afternoon sun which had now moved to a westerly position in the cloudless sky dazzled her eyes and warmed her exposed arms, legs, and neck. She put on her sunglasses and looked around her, all the while being buffeted by the excited crowd of people behind her who were anxious to get to the beach on this warm sunny Sunday, the last holiday weekend of the summer.

Almost all of the day trippers turned right from the station exit, which was the shortest way to the small stretch of sandy beach that lay just outside the wall of the small harbour at the mouth of the river Dargle. Most of the Bray sea shore was pebbles but the north end of the prom contained a sandy portion which was popular with swimmers and those wishing to lie around or bath and splash in the water, but Lesley, after a moment's hesitation turned left and made her way towards the narrow laneway just across the road from the station. She had brought her swimsuit but decided to wait till later in the afternoon when the beach would be less crowded, to venture into the water. It seemed she was the only one not in a hurry to get to the beach because as she stood and looked around before proceeding down the lane she was all alone, everyone it seemed had headed beachside.

Most of Lesley's life had been spent in America though she had been born in Ireland but shortly after her birth, when she was less than two years old her parents emigrated and her father had become an American cop. Although now totally American in mind and spirit she had been raised on tales of Ireland and her father had very often spoken about his childhood and the many summer days he had spent in Bray which is why she knew where all the day trippers were headed and why she decided to wait till later to visit the beach.

She was back in Ireland with her mother to scatter her father's ashes here. Seamus Bannister, her father had been killed in a shootout on the streets of Queens, New York, over ten years ago when she was only a teenager but this was the first time they had made it back to Ireland to carry out his wishes. She missed her father so much and always regretted that she had got to spend so little time with him before he was gunned down. She also regretted that he had become a cop and was in danger of dying every time he went to work.

She remembered that day so well, she had only turned eighteen and was becoming increasingly aware of how dangerous a job her fathers was. Every night it seemed there was an item on the television news about a cop being injured or killed and one night it was her father who made the headlines.

A few days before the killing she had blown out the candles on her eighteenth birthday cake and made a wish. It was that her father had never become a cop, that he had never emigrated to America and had stayed instead in Ireland the land he loved, impossible and all as that wish was then. She had been mesmerised by his stories of Ireland and always regretted she would never hear his broad Dublin accent enthralling her with his tales again. He had made Albert Walk, which she now realized was a narrow dismal laneway with a few strings of old broken festive lights still hanging across its narrow expanse sound so magical when he spoke of it and Lesley had wasted no time in visiting it when she arrived in Bray.

But what she found herself looking at now was an undistinguished walkway no more than ten or twelve feet wide with a row of shop fronts on the right side as you proceeded in the direction of Bray Head and on the left side the back entrances to houses.   Its glory days were long over now it seemed but she remembered her father telling her tales from his childhood when it was the main artery taken to the beach by the day trippers arriving at the station from the city and was always full of people and packed shops selling ice cream, candy floss and all kinds of cheap holiday novelties as well as quaint tea rooms and amusement arcades, fortune tellers, and even a cinema.

It had sounded so attractive and exciting to her as he told it but as she now stood at the entrance to the walk it was just a nondescript deserted laneway except for a lone busker in a cowboy hat who obviously disliked an audience as he had it seemed picked the most deserted spot in Bray to ply his trade and he was singing to himself.

She remembered her dad telling her of how exciting a place it used to be to the young Dublin urchin that he was in those depressed years of his childhood and how he looked forward with excited anticipation to visiting the seaside resort on the few times a year he raised the train fare to do so. He spoke of the overpowering smell of fish and chips that used permeate the air and the gambling emporiums, or more accurately the slot machine premise that he was forbidden entry to but somehow always managed to evade the attention of the doorman and lose his few pence to the one armed bandits.

Those simple pleasures were all gone now as the modern day tripper had acquired more sophisticated tastes and had no need it seemed for plastic novelties such as buckets and spades and bamboo fishing nets or slot machines with fifty pence jackpots. Most of the shop fronts were shuttered now too with 'For Sale' or 'To Let' notices on them and the few premises still doing business were not exactly overflowing with customers, still there was a certain old world charm about the place that she liked as she closed her eyes and tried to imagine it as it used to be and as described by her father as he tried to bring to life again the happy days of his childhood that he left behind when he emigrated to America and gave his life for his new homeland.

In a way she was glad it was not like it used to be back then when her father was a child as she casually took her time in walking the length of the lane in peace without the hustle and bustle of crowds. Half way down the lane or to give it its proper nomenclature, Albert Walk, she noticed a small coffee shop still open with a small round wrought iron table covered in red and white check lino and two wooden chairs outside. It had a half lace curtain strung across its large window very similar to how some premises used to be decorated in the past but nothing to indicate it was still open apart from an out of date menu taped to the window beside a 'Help Wanted' notice, though why help was needed escaped her as it was so quiet. It looked so out of place, or maybe it was exactly in place and in keeping with how the walk used to be as its owner had made no attempt to modernize the premises and it looked exactly as she remembered her father's descriptions of the premises on the Walk and how they used to look. She sat on one of the chairs and waited to be served and when after five or six minutes no one had come to take her order, and it certainly was not because they were too busy, she stood up and entered the shop.

She was amazed at what she saw, the shop was packed with people and there was a buzz of conversation and laughter that she had not heard when she was sitting outside. She stood just inside the door and in a state of total amazement observed a room full of people having teas and scones and laughing and joking and children running around and playing with plastic windmills and bamboo fishing nets and jam jars on string containing small fish and baby crabs.

No one took the slightest bit of notice of her as she stood looking at the scene before her and it was as if she was invisible. As she took in the scene she heard a voice above the babble of voices that predominated in the room.

'Be with you in a minute lady, there's a table just becoming
vacant now'
Lesley looked to where the voice had spoken from and she
froze.
No, no, that was not possible, it could not be, nobody------, but
as she looked closely at the boy who had called to her she was
struck by the uncanny resemblance, the amazing resemblance
even to how he looked at that age.

'Seamus, Seamus, are you coming or what?'
Thomas Russell called up at the open window in the tenement
building that was home to Seamus Bannister in the north
inner city of Dublin.
'Yea, I'll be down in a minute I just have to get me jacket'
Seamus replied and pulled the window shut and still putting
on his corduroy zip jacket which he was wearing over the Levi
jeans he had purchased for thirty shillings in Power and
Moore's in Talbot Street, ran down the six flights of wooden
stairs and opened the heavy wooden door of the tenement.
'Come on quick the train is in ten minutes, if we miss that one
the next is not for an hour' Thomas said as they both ran as
fast as they could in the direction of the train station at the end
of Talbot Street.
'How much have you got?' Thomas asked as they ran through
the crowded streets leading to the station, narrowly avoiding
bumping into people as they hurried to catch the train.
'Two and six is all I have. I had to get a new pair of jeans
yesterday so that's all I have left. I hope the oul fellah on the
ticket desk does not ask me me age'
'Scouch down and tell him you're only fourteen and he won't
notice'
'How much have you?' Seamus asked.
'Five Bob, and I nicked two bob of that from me oul fellahs
pocket when he was asleep' 'Jasus Tommo what will you do if
he finds out?'

'He won't, he was drinking last night and he'll think he spent it so he will. Anyway if he had it he'd only spend it tonight. I'm doing me ma a favour so I am, he's an awful bollocks when he gets drunk. I'm never going to drink. Great we'll make it we're there' Thomas then said as they reached the station and proceeded to run up the steep flight of steps that led to the main concourse.

'A child's return ticket to Bray please' Seamus said as he slid the two shilling coin under the glass panel of the ticket desk. 'A child's ticket? How old are you young fella' the ticket clerk asked but at the same time issued the ticket and slid back the change. Seamus did not answer the question, he just took the change and ticket and said, 'Thanks mister'
The same procedure ensued when Thomas bought his ticket and with the tickets safely in their pockets the pair ran to the train with seconds to spare and squeezed into an already full carriage and with a smile to each other sighed with relief as they began the journey to Bray.

An hour later they were in the resort of Bray and itching to sample its exotic mix of ice cream parlours, slot machine venues, carnival's, paddle boats and best of all the chair lift up the side of Bray Head.

'I only have one and nine left' Seamus said 'that's not enough to do all I want to do. Will we go to the slots first so that I can win a few bob?'
'Ah for fuck sake Seamus you know you won't win anything, you'll end up losing the few pence you have'
'Well what will I do? This won't go far in Bray'
As they were discussing their financial position they were already walking down Albert Walk and as they passed a tea room Thomas looked at Seamus and pointed to a notice stuck on the window.
'Waiters Wanted' it said.

'There's the solution, we'll get a job'
'Are you gone mad or something, get a job? Sure we're only here for the day'
'Yea and we'll only work for the day, well work for a few hours anyway and then make an almighty mess of things and we'll be paid off and we'll have plenty of money to spend until the last train leaves tonight'
Seamus looked at Thomas and thought about it, looked at the few coins in his hand and said, 'Do you think we'd get away with that?'
'We can try can't we' Thomas replied and smiled.
Very gingerly they entered the tea room and asked to speak to the manager who turned out to be a tall well built American gentleman.
'Eh are you still looking for waiters?' Thomas asked, 'if you are can we have the jobs-----please?
'Are you a waiter?' The man replied in an intimidating American accent and Thomas looked at Seamus and Seamus looked at the man who was at least four inches taller than he was and replied, 'Yea, yea we are'
'Where have you worked, where have you waited?' the yank asked them in a thick New York drawl.
'Eh, eh we've, we've--------'
Seamus stammered and started to move away from the man.
'I'm thinking the only waiting you two have done is wait for a bus' the man replied and as they made to leave the cafe the man said,   'If
you want a job, and because I'm stuck I'll let you work for the afternoon and if you are suitable-----well we'll see'
'Thanks mister' they both said together, 'that would be great'
And so Seamus and Thomas instead of gallivanting around Bray for the afternoon found themselves serving tea, sandwiches and scones to respectable ladies and gentlemen in a tea room on Albert Walk.

Two weeks later Seamus was still waiting on tables in the tea room but Thomas had tired of the job and left. The season was fast approaching its end and Seamus was almost sorry. For the last four or five weeks he had really enjoyed his time in the tea room and the money he had earned had been a great boost to his morale, having a few bob in his pocket had boosted his confidence no end and he had formed a good relationship with the owner who he learned was a former New York city cop of Irish descent who had decided to take his pension and retire to the land of his ancestors.

As the last holiday weekend of the summer approached and Mike Roche announced a closing date for the cafe, he was returning to the states for a few months to see old friends and colleagues he told the staff, he took Seamus aside and asked what he would do when he was laid off in a few weeks time. Seamus had no plan's, he would just fall back into his old ways and probably take up again with Thomas he told Mike.
'Ever think of joining the cops? The American cops Shay' Mike asked.
Seamus hadn't but Mike had planted an idea in his head.
'If you ever consider it I could be of some help, I think my name still counts for something back in Queens' he said.
Seamus said he would consider it as there was no real opportunities for someone like him, someone with little education and from the inner city tenements of Dublin in Ireland in those depressed times and besides he had got used to being able to jingle a few bob in his pocket.
He had also recently begun to see and court a girl he met in Bray.

One evening after he had finished his shift and was sitting eating his fish supper on the prom while he waited for his train he met Alison. It was a fine warm evening and the sea was calm with just about enough energy in the faint sounding gentle swish of the waves to disturb the stones on the sea shore when he noticed her. She was very attractive he thought and he wished he had had the courage to approach her but she was not taking any notice of him. She was alone and eating an ice cream cone. As she sat eating and seemingly enjoying her cone a dog bounded up the prom and playfully jumped up at her and knocked the cone from her hand. Seamus being the gentleman he was and also seeing the opportunity he wanted to get to speak to her approached her and said he had seen what had happened and as he was about to buy himself a cone could he also get her a fresh one too? At first she did not respond to his presence as it seemed she was still a bit shocked from the encounter with the dog but when he asked again she smiled at him and said,
'Sorry for being so distracted but that dog gave me an awful fright and I was really enjoying that cone'
'Yes I could see that. So then, can I get you another one?' he smiled at her and she relaxed and smiled back,
'Would you? Yes please, that would be nice'
They sat together talking until it was time for the last train and then they headed to the station and got the last train back to the city together and he walked her to her home which it turned out was not that far from where he lived, thou not a tenement, and in the time he had spent with her he found her so easy to talk to that he actually found the courage to ask if he could see her again.

Seamus often wished he could have thanked that dog for its intervention into his life because the relationship with Alison developed over time into a full blown romance and when the Tea Rooms closed and Mike went back to America Seamus continued to see Alison and their love deepened and then when Summer came round again and Mike returned and reopened the Tea Rooms Seamus began working for him again and told him about Alison and asked if he had meant it when he spoke of helping him become an American cop.

That was three years ago and he believed that if he had a permanent job with prospects, like being a cop, he could see possibilities in he and Alison-------well his future was looking good from where he stood now.
He spoke to Mike a few times after that about what he had said about becoming a cop and from what Mike told him he believed it was a job he could handle and be good at, especially if he had a good woman by his side.

His relationship with Alison over time had developed into a full blown passionate love affair and he had no doubt that she was the woman he wanted to spend the rest of his life with and raise a family with, so he spoke to her about his conversations with Mike and what he had been telling him about life as an American cop and Alison came on board with the idea.

Before the last holiday weekend of his third year with Mike he asked Alison to marry him and she accepted and plans were put in train for the wedding after which they intended with Mike's help to emigrate to America. Then Alison discovered she was pregnant.

It should not have been a surprise, they were madly in love and------well they had been doing what lovers do,-------- every chance they got. Still it was a bit of a hindrance to their plans, they had intended emigrating shortly after the wedding but now, well the families became involved and especially Alison's parents. They were insisting that they put off going to America until after the birth of the baby. In actual fact Alison and Seamus kinda felt the same way, they wanted their child born in Ireland and after further discussions with Mike it was decided that they would wait till after the birth of their baby before they set off for America.

While these plans were awaiting fulfillment Seamus with Mike's help managed to secure employment that helped keep the wolf from the door after they were married but Seamus knew it would always be like this if he remained in Ireland, a few weeks work here a few more there and money always a problem and so before Lesley, it was a girl they had and they called her Lesley, was two years of age they said goodbye to their friends and family in Dublin and set off for a new life in America. While that life had been a good life it suddenly all came to an end when Seamus was killed in a street battle with a gang of hoodlums when Lesley was still in her teens.

'This way Miss I've a table for you over here' the boy said as he led Lesley through the crowded room. Lesley was in a daze as she followed the boy.

'There you are, nice and snug and away from the draught of the door, even on warm days like this there can be a terrible draught from that door' he said.

'Thank you, thank you this is fine' Lesley replied still unable to take her eyes off the boy.

'You're an American then? On holidays here?' the boy asked on hearing her accent.

'Yes, yes I am, though I was actually born here in Ireland, in the Rotunda in fact'

'Well fancy that now, I'd never have guessed with that accent'

'Yes well its true, I'm a true blue Dub with an American accent' Lesley replied and smiled, now a bit more relaxed.

'Have you ever been to the States?' she asked the boy.

'No not yet but I hope to go there someday. My boss, the man who owns this place, Mike Roche is a yank and he was telling me about the place, it sounds great'

'My God' Lesley thought, 'Mike Roche! This is not happening, it can't be'

She had often heard her parents talk about Mike Roche, the man who was responsible for her father going to the States and becoming a cop but she had never met him.

'Anyway what can I get you, I'm afraid we don't have the selection of food you might be used to in America, sandwiches and cakes I'm afraid, but we do have coffee, real coffee!' the boy said.

'A coffee and apple pie, if you have it, will be fine thanks' Lesley replied and felt her eyes well up with tears as her mind went back to her eighteenth birthday and the wish she had made. She wished her father had never become a cop and would thus not have been in America to be gunned down on the streets of Queens. Was this the chance to make that wish come true she thought as she sat waiting for her coffee and apple pie.

Then the boy came back and placed her food on the table and said, 'There you are lady, apple pie and a real coffee, this is one of the few places in Ireland you'll get real coffee, Mike gets the beans from a supplier in New York and we grind them here'

Lesley looked at the boy and as he stood smiling at her she took his hand in hers and said, 'Please Seamus, please don't ever go to America no matter what Mike Roche tells you'

The boy looked at Lesley and withdrew his hand from hers and asked,

'How do you know my name? Who are you, why are you here?'

He asked totally bewildered at what was happening. This lady who had only now walked into the cafe-----how did she know his name?

'I asked you how do you know my name lady? Is this some kind of joke set up by Mike, after all you are both yanks and maybe you think it's great fun to make a fool of the poor Irish yokel, is that it?'

'No, no I don't know what's happening either------dad' Lesley replied 'but I do know that mother, Alison, the girl you will soon marry is at this moment pregnant, she is carrying me in her womb'

Seamus literally felt his heart stop beating and he fell into a chair and the blood drained from his face on hearing the words Lesley had spoken.

'Please dad, please Seamus I came here because of the stories you told me when I was------when I was young back in Queens, in New York'

'I never told you stories, I was never in New York' The boy replied

'Yes you did dad. And I wished you had never become a cop and gone to America because----because-----oh dad oh dad please don't go to America. How is this possible dad, how did I come to walk into this tea room and find you when you're----?'

All at once Lesley heard her name being called and she turned and standing at the door was her father and mother.

'Come on Lesley our train is in five minutes, we better go' her father said and as Lesley turned back to the young boy he was gone and the tea room had taken on a different aspect. It was now almost empty, only her and a woman having a cup of tea.

As Lesley looked around the old tea room, which was now almost empty and bore no resemblance to the room she was in a moment ago she tried to understand what had just happened and only then noticed an old framed picture on the wall, it showed her father when he was a young man with Mike Roche and other staff members standing outside the premises smiling into the camera. Her father then joined her and pointing to the picture on the wall put his arm around her, kissed her on the cheek and said,

'Don't you just love Bray and Albert Walk, a magical place. Nowhere else could you walk into an old tea room that should have been shut down years ago and find on the wall a picture of yourself on the very day you made the most momentous decision of your life. That picture was taken on the day I told Mike Roche I was not going to go to America and join the cops. I'm so glad I made that decision. I was so close to going, but it must have been someone's special wish that saved me from going' and he squeezed Lesley's hand and winked at her.

The Last Banshee

Dexter Robbins best days as a leading man were over and the scripts were scarce these days but even so he had not exactly jumped at the chance to come to Ireland where apparently he was still held in some measure of esteem to play a starring role in a new horror film, 'The Last Banshee'
'Where the hell is Ardmore Studios anyway' he asked his agent when he gave him the script and reminded him that he had not been doing that very often in recent years.
'They're in Ireland, in some town called Bray outside Dublin' Ted Maxwell replied.
'Ted may I remind you that I've never played in a horror film before, my genera is romance and high class drama, that's the kind of roles my fans expect and are used to'
'Dexter may I remind you that you haven't played in any kind of film recently. When was the last time you played in either of those genera's? Besides your fans are few and far between these days, they are nearly all as old as you are yourself and dropping off the shelf of life fast, so I suggest you make at least one more film for them while someone is still willing to offer you money to do so'
Dexter Robbins looked at his agent and then at his own reflection in the mirror in Teds office and knew that Ted was right.

It had been at least five years since he had been offered a new script and he could not guess how many years since he was last on a working movie set, apart from a few guest appearances on cheap television shows. He was well past the point of him being a heartthrob now but he still looked good for his age, six feet two in height, all his own teeth, true he was just beginning to show a paunch but he still had most of his dark brown hair, even if it was dark brown with a little aid from his hairdresser. If he rejected this script when he wondered would he get the chance to reject another one. He ran the page edges of the script across his finger tips and sighed,

'When does shooting begin?'

'That's my boy Dexter' Ted replied and smiled 'Make it one for the Gipper'

Dexter was met at the airport by the director of the film Lucy O'Connor. Lucy was a recent graduate of some film production course and this was to be her directorial debut which when he found out did not go down too well with Dexter. Being reduced to playing in a horror film was bad enough but now he was at the mercy of some novice director. Let's just do this and get the hell back to Hollywood he thought.

'I'm so pleased that you could find the time to come to Ireland and make this film Mr. Robbins' Lucy said as she over enthusiastically shook Dexter's hand in the V.I.P. lounge of the airport as a battery of reporters and cameramen captured the moment a member of Hollywood royalty came to Ireland to make a film based on the memoir of a descendent of the reputed last Banshee to have existed and to be directed by her great granddaughter.

'So where am I staying while shooting this movie?' Dexter asked Lucy as he had requested that he be accommodated in his own apartment and not a hotel while shooting the film, and that it be close to the studio as well. He didn't want a hotel because he didn't want to be the subject of prying eyes and annoying fans every time he went to the bar or restaurant, he was here to work not discuss his career with inquisitive pests . Lucy had she believed fulfilled those requests and replied as they drove away from the airport in a chauffeur driven limo as the cameras continued to capture them,

'I did my research and I know how good a professional you are Mr. Robbins and I know how you like to get into the spirit of the character when working so we have had the former home of the real life character you will be playing in this film refurbished and it is there you will be staying'

'I see' Dexter replied not knowing how he should interpret that statement. Lucy picking up on his somewhat ambiguous reply then said,

'Oh its very comfortable and you will have all the assistance you require regarding cooking and living facilities. Everything is laid on for you, a valet will be provided with a daily cleaning service for you and it's near the studio'

Dexter did not reply but looked at Lucy closely for the first time since arriving, at the airport there was too many distractions with the introductions and all the reporters and the television and radio interviews to be done but now as they motored away from the airport he scrutinised her closely. About thirty he reckoned, auburn hair worn loose, little if any make up apart from lipstick and a faint coating of eye liner which tended to highlight her large attractive hazel eyes and from where he was sitting a good figure and shapely legs which she had at that moment crossed exposing some flesh on her inner thigh.

'I've read the script Lucy, may I call you Lucy?' Dexter at last spoke, 'and despite the fact that I have never played in a horror film before, you know how it is 'real' actors tend to shy away from such things, but things being as they are now in La La land most actors of my-----vintage let us say, tend to be less choosey. But may I say it reads good, very good in fact. How much of it is------well you did say it was based on a memoir, how much of it is tr-real and how much is fiction?'

'Yes of course call me Lucy, that's my name, and it's all real----Dexter?'

'Good I like it when we are on first name terms I find it easier to work that way. You would not believe how many ass holes there are in Hollywood who insist on being addressed as Mr. this or Mr. that. All ego and no talent. So Lucy, it's all real you say and how do you know----I mean if you use that line of marketing to promote the film you can be sure some reporters will be only too eager to blow that assertion out of the water, look what they did to that recent phenomena 'found footage'

'It's all true Dexter have no doubt about that, I've wanted to make this film for decades and no amount of huffing and puffing by inquisitive newshounds will blow this house away'

Dexter looked at Lucy and smiled. Although she may be a novice as regards her experience he could see that she was a strong and determined woman and he was looking forward to working with her, now that he was getting to know her.

Presently they reached their destination and the chauffer got out and opened the door. Lucy got out first and then Dexter stepped out of the car.

'This is where------where the character you will be playing used to live Dexter. I'll walk you to the door. It's too narrow for the car to get any nearer. I'm sure you'll want to relax and unwind after your trip and besides I have a meeting to attend. There's food and drink already prepared for you and the place is stocked with all you will need and I'll pick you up tomorrow for breakfast and then take you to the studios, they are not far from here and you can meet the cast and we can start our work on the film then'

As Lucy led him down the narrow lane followed by the chauffer with Dexter's luggage Dexter noticed an old stone marker with the name Albert Walk engraved on it. 'Sounds like a soap opera' he thought to himself. At the door of the apartment he was to stay in Lucy inserted a key into the lock and opened the door revealing a small hallway and a flight of stairs. She handed him the key and said

'Welcome to Bray Dexter, I hope your time here will be very happy and be the launching of a new career------for us both' And with that she smiled at him and went back to the car to await the chauffer who proceeded to carry Dexter's luggage up the stairs.

Dexter thanked Lucy and watched her as she went back to the car and the chauffer brought his luggage up the flight of stairs to the apartment which appeared to be over a shop of some description. Not exactly what he had in mind but it was late and he would wait till the morning to make his feelings known. He tipped the chauffer and closed the door of the apartment. He began inspecting his new home and after a thorough inspection decided that he liked what he saw even if he had began to have misgivings when he first saw his new abode. Most of the furnishings were solid wood and the ornaments, to his uneducated eyes antiques. It was quite a change from the Bling of Hollywood but at this stage of his career he quite liked that, this was a real apartment meant for living in, not a quasi stage set that was the norm back in tinsel town. He went to the small window and pulled back the curtain and for the first time felt a bit disappointed. All that was visible was a narrow dark laneway and although it was quite late and there was no one about there was a busker quietly singing to himself half way down the lane.
'Welcome to Albert Walk' he said to himself 'I sure hope Albert has a flashlight when he goes walking in that dark lane'
     As he stood letting his eyes get accustomed to the dark outside his window he noticed a faint cloud of what seemed like white smoke drifting in the wind to his left and as his eyes accustomed themselves to the faint light from some building also to his left he heard the unmistakable sound of an old steam train engine.

'There must be a rail line near here' he thought 'and by the sound of it they still have steam locomotives. I wonder how far away it is'

He tried to open the window to get a better look at his surroundings but it was stuck solid and would not budge.

'I better get Lucy to get someone to free this window tomorrow, I doubt if this apartment has air conditioning and fresh air would be nice'

He toyed with the idea of going out and finding the rail line and having a look at the steam locomotive, something he had not seen since his childhood, but decided that maybe he should wait till tomorrow when it was bright, after all he didn't want to go out and lose his way in a town he was unacquainted with. He'd speak to Lucy tomorrow and she'd tell him all about the town and where to find the train station.

Boy it would be great to take a trip in one of those old steam locomotives again he thought. That settled he continued his tour of the apartment and he found the fridge in the other room and it was well stocked with booze he was glad to see so instead of going out he kicked off his shoes and poured himself a large, a very large whiskey and sat in an old well upholstered armchair and drank his whiskey.

When he was relaxed and all warmed inside by the whiskey he felt his eyes grow heavy and he fell into a deep sleep which was facilitated by the sounds of the steam locomotives as they came and went from the nearby station.

At two thirty in the morning his sleep was disturbed by what sounded like a blood curdling scream and he sat bolt upright in the chair and in a state of shock and panic ran to the window thinking there may have been some kind of locomotive accident but there was no sign of any unusual activity. But as he scanned the lane to his surprise he saw the figure of a woman, at least he assumed it was a woman because of the old fashioned long skirt and hat it was wearing, standing at the corner to Albert Walk looking at the apartment and when Dexter pulled back the curtain to get a better look there was a loud whistle of a locomotive and a mighty discharge of smoke billowed from around the corner which completely enveloped the figure and completely obliterated his view and when the smoke cleared the woman was gone.

'Good morning Dexter' Lucy said as he opened the door to her, 'I hope you slept well last night, we have a busy day ahead of us. I've scheduled a meeting with cast and crew in the studio so we can all get to know each other. But first I'll take you for breakfast, there's a few nice little restaurants along the sea front we can go to, one in particular I like and I'm sure you'll like it too'

'Hi Lucy' Dexter replied 'I'm in your hands so that sounds good to me. But before we head to the studio I'd sure like to see one of those old steam locomotives you guys still have working here, by the sounds they were making last night the station must be very close by'

'Steam locomotives?' Lucy enquired, 'The train station is just around the corner but it's been quite a long time since steam trains ran on the tracks'

'They were running last night, damn it they woke me from my sleep. I heard them loud and clear and saw the steam they were discharging' Dexter replied and as Lucy looked at him uneasily he said,

'Now wait just a minute young lady, I was not hallucinating, I only had---well not enough drink to do that to my mind and I heard the unmistakable sound of old steam locomotives running close by here last night. I have no idea where the station is in this town but they sure were close, close enough for me to see the steam they were discharging'

'Dexter no steam train has run on the Bray line in at least oh, sixty years or more. We have what we call The Dart and that's an electric powered system, there's no steam discharged'

'Lucy I'm telling you I hea-------'
Then a smile came to his face as he looked at Lucy and said, 'I get it. You said you did your research on me and know that I like to get into character for each part I'm playing and since this is a horror film you and the crew were priming me for the part. Very clever I must say. And that woman I saw in the lane and the blood curdling sound, all part of your little game'

'Dexter I have no idea what you are talking about. I nor as far as I am aware, and I know my crew, no one is playing games with you. What you saw or think you saw last night has absolutely nothing to do with me nor anyone associated with this film'

'Ah fuck this Lucy I was not imagining what happened last night, I was wide awake and I distinctly heard the sound of steam trains and saw the smoke, I stood at that window and--, oh by the way can you get someone to prize it open, its stuck solid and I like the feel of fresh air in my nostrils'

As Dexter said this Lucy went to the window and with ease opened it saying,

'Everything was fixed and refurbished in the apartment for you Dexter'

'Lucy last night that window-----that----- Ah fuck it come on let's get breakfast and get this show on the road'
Dexter said somewhat annoyed by what he had experienced and what Lucy had said and he tried to dismiss it from his mind.

The sea air and the early morning sun and the walkers and joggers on the long prom which stretched from a small harbour to the magnificent vista of Bray Head went some way to calming Dexter's anxiety about his first night in Ireland and his -------well whatever had caused him to see and hear what he experienced last night.

After putting away a full Irish breakfast of bacon, eggs, sausage, black and white pudding, which he loved and had second helpings of, and coffee and toast he was in a more relaxed mood and after smoking a cigarette he asked Lucy,

'This guy whom I'm playing and in whose apartment I'm staying, who exactly was he? I have read the script but that's just a script, in real life I mean, who was he?'

Lucy drained the last of her coffee and then looked down towards Bray Head as the bright sun moved slowly southerly towards it and replied,

'He was my great grandmother's lover. He was a Banshee hunter who fell in love with a Banshee, the last Banshee, who happened to be my great grandmother'

Dexter took a long hard pull on his cigarette and said,

'Wow that's some opening statement Lucy I gotta hear the rest of the story'

'That's a heavy tale Lucy, really heavy' Dexter said when Lucy had told him the story of the love affair between the Banshee hunter and her great grandmother the last Banshee.

'So you are the direct descendent of a Banshee? Is that correct?'

'Yes, I'm an O'Connor and the O'Connor's are one of the legendary families the Banshee attached themselves to in the dim distant past when they were being hunted in Ireland, that's why I want to make this film. The Banshee has had a 'bad press 'as you would say in America. For centuries she was depicted as the harbinger of death and I want to set the record straight and tell the real story.

The Banshee Lucy explained goes right back to Biblical times, they were the progeny of the daughters of men that the sons of the Gods found so attractive that they mated with them and for that sin of their parents they were hunted across the face of the earth until they could go no further. In Ireland they reached the end of the Earth, there was nowhere else for them to go. And in Ireland they were hunted to extinction'

'That's quite a story Lucy, but not quite true is it?' Lucy looked at Dexter with surprise and asked,

'What do you mean by that, there are no more Banshees. My great grandmother was-----'.

Before Lucy could finish her sentence Dexter interjected, 'The Banshee was not hunted to extinction' he said, 'you----- well you being the great granddaughter of ------does that not make you---a Banshee?'

Lucy smiled at him and said, 'That's very perceptive of you Dexter and it would be true if my inherited DNA had not been contaminated over the centuries. I no longer have the pure genes of the Gods that entitles me to call myself a Banshee. I am an O'Connor, one of the old Irish families the Banshee attached themselves to and men like my Great Grandmother's lover mated with. I do not have the pure genes nor the wisdom of the Banshee that so many of my ancestors were hunted and slaughtered for having. The Banshee no longer exist Dexter' Lucy replied with a tone of finality in her voice.

Dexter was silent for a few moments as they both contemplated what had been said and then he said, 'As you say Lucy, but did----did your great grandmother, did she live with her lover----the Banshee hunter,---- in the apartment?'

Lucy looked at him and with a wistful sound in her voice replied,   'No, no they could not risk that, but she visited him when he---, well he was a priest, and it was primarily the church who hunted the Banshee, and the apartment was their hideaway and when he was there she travelled from her sanctuary in Wexford to visit him. Why, why do you ask that?'

'I don't know, but what happened last night----Lucy it was real I swear to you I heard the sounds of steam trains and if as you say steam trains have not run on that line for decades then----Lucy there was a woman outside the apartment last night, standing on the corner of Albert Walk. She was rigged out in old fashioned clothes, I saw her when I went to the window and.----is it possible she was-------your great grandmother?---- that is, well could there have been a -----a time slip and----your grandmother, the Banshee, could I have seen her visit her lover?'

Lucy smiled at him and said, 'I don't think so Dexter, things like that, as you well know, only happen in the movies'

The Virgins Revenge

Another Saturday night and the crowds were leaving the Arcadia Ballroom, most of them as couples but Joyce Jennings was alone as usual. She had gone to the dance alone too, something she was used to by now though she had met some friends there but she was leaving alone as she had not got a leave home,---- again.

It's not that she was unattractive, she wasn't, she was a very good looking and well built twenty five year old young blond lady that any man you would think would be proud and happy to make love to, but for some strange reason she was still a virgin.

She worked as a solicitor's secretary in a large legal practice on the main street of Bray and it was no secret that she had a huge crush on her boss Richard Mansfield SC. Problem was Richard was a thirty something handsome married man.

A very handsome man indeed and a senior partner in the firm and who knew only too well his effect on Joyce and the rest of the females in the office but always remained aloof and out of reach to the mere females who swooned and lusted for his attention and he had never shown any interest in an extra marital affair with Joyce or indeed with any of the other girls in the office, most of whom would have made themselves available at the drop of the merest hint that Richard was interested. Joyce reckoned he could have had his pick of the flock, including her.

And some of the 'emancipated' women made no secret of the fact that they were available should he be so inclined and to hell with his wife. He was always courteous and mannerly towards Joyce and treated her with the utmost respect, but she so wished he would just once drop the altar boy persona and show some of the red blooded passion she suspected lurked beneath the cool surface and that he was ready and willing to deflower her because she was blooming and just waiting to be pruned.

She stood at the corner of Albert Walk just a bit away from the ballroom in the hope of getting a taxi before the crowds standing around the entrance to the dance hall began to disperse and take the few taxis that were available. A few taxis passed her in favour of more lucrative fares, after all two paid twice as much as one.

After about a half hour's wait and no taxi she decided she would have to walk home, home was not that far, just up beyond New Court Road down towards the Head but at this time of night, or more correctly morning as it was now well past midnight, it was not something she liked doing alone.

No point in waiting any longer she decided and began walking down Albert Walk. As she proceeded down the lane with Richard not a million miles from her mind, how she wished she was walking home with him, she got the surprise of her life. A door opened and -----well she was not prepared for what she saw.

Richard Mansfield emerged and as he did he turned just as she was past the door and embraced a young man of about nineteen or twenty and planted a passionate kiss on his lips. He had not seen her, she was sure of that because he just turned and proceeded in the opposite direction to her after he took his pleasure but she was shaking and in a state of shock at what she had seen.

Richard Mansfield was a homosexual! Her mind went into a tizzy and she did not know what to do, run after him or run home and try to put into perspective what she had seen. In a trance she just continued walking almost on auto pilot and let her legs take her where they would because she certainly was not consciously directing them to where they were going.

How would she ever face him on Monday morning knowing now what she knew, Joyce wondered. Everything had changed, her whole world was changed.
Her fantasy lover was no more. She eventually made it home but her legs felt like jelly, not because of the walk but because of what she now knew. Who would ever have guessed? Richard Mansfield, every woman in the office's idea of the perfect ride, a puff!
Then she started to laugh. All this time she had been fantasizing of him taking her in his arms and stripping her bare and making love to her until they were both exhausted and could barely breath, but the chances of that happening were about as good as winning the lottery without buying a ticket she now realized.
Still she would have to face him on Monday morning and how could she do that with a straight face knowing what she now knew.

She went to mass the next morning and who did she see up near the front of the church, where all the pillars of the community sat and prayed, all the better to having their prayers heard and answered by the Deity before the common crowd got a word in, but the bould Richard. His wife Elizabeth was not with him, how significant was that she wondered. Poor Elizabeth she thought, imagine going to bed with that Adonis every night and not being able to raise his spear-----oh Joyce she said to herself, stop it, not in the church!

She left the vicinity of the church before the great and the good came out and took a walk along the prom and after a cup of coffee in a tea room made her way back towards the scene of her discovery last night. She walked the length of Albert Walk and stopped casually outside the door she saw Richard and his boyfriend kiss goodnight and tried to imagine it was her he was kissing.

All day she could not get the sight of 'The Kiss' out of her mind and she wondered if Elizabeth knew. Of course she knew! How could she not know? Why were a young married couple like them apart on a Saturday night, where did she think he was?

Where did he tell her he was? Then. Where was she?

After an uneasy afternoon and evening thinking of Richard and his boyfriend and the things they might get up to she wondered if the church was open on Sunday evening so that she could go to confession in case she died during the night.

Monday morning eventually came and Joyce arose from her bed in a bedroom she shared with her older spinster sister, two virgins in the one bedroom probably constituted half the total population of the virgins in Bray she thought and now with Richard out of the deflower the virgin stakes the chances of that changing in the near future were as good as guaranteed not to happen. After a breakfast of cereal and fruit juice prepared by her widowed mother she departed for the office.

She decided to walk as she still was in a quandary about how she would react when she saw Richard and she wanted to delay that moment as long as possible. However, all moments of decision eventually arrive and Joyce's came sooner than she thought it would. She had taken the scenic route to the office and as she walked up from the prom towards the main street near the train station Richard was walking out of Albert Walk. He stopped to put a few coins into the hat of Gerry Sullivan the busker who plied his trade in Albert Walk and as he adjusted his coat after taking the money from his pocket and making his contribution to Gerry's war on want fund he saw her.

'Hello Joyce' he called 'on the way to the office?'

'Oh hello Richard, yes, yes on the way to another week of fantasizing that you might want to ride me only now I know that I'd have to have a prick before that would happen' she didn't say but instead said 'Yes Richard all set for another week of straightening out legal entanglements. Did you have a good weekend?'

'Yes I did, I had a very good weekend' he replied with a big smile on his face.

'I'll bet you had, you and your toy boy, does Elizabeth know where your prick was this weekend?' she thought but instead said 'That's good, did you and Elizabeth go somewhere nice?'

'Eh no, no we--I mean Elizabeth---Elizabeth went to her mother's place in Clare, she's not well you know. Her mother I mean is not well Elizabeth is fine' he stammered

How convenient, while the cats away the mouse will play she thought.

'Oh I'm sorry to hear that, and you how did you ------I mean what did you do all on your own for the weekend?'

He ignored the question and instead looked at his watch and said,

'My goodness look at the time, we better get a move on or we'll be late, and arriving in late together might give some the wrong idea of how we spent the weekend' and smiled at his attempt at humour.

Joyce looked at him with a knowing grin and said,
'That would never do at all Richard would it? Although some people might already have the wrong idea of how you spend your weekends. If you know what I mean, which I'm sure you do'

She was being brazen now but she had just had her fantasy about Richard shattered, a fantasy that was a consolation for her hanging on to her virginity for so long and hoping he would be the one to take it which she knew was never going to happen now and so she decided to have her revenge. She still fancied him big time despite what she knew and still wanted him to be the one to take her virginity, which she was sure would still be possible with a little help from her.

Richard looked at her in a quizzical way and said,
'I really don't know what you mean Joyce, that's a strange thing to say'

This was it, it was now or never, as Elvis might say. Her virginity was on the line and had been hanging there waving to Richard for too long now.

'Does Elizabeth know about------well about your little peccadillo?'

'My what?' Richard replied 'what are you talking about?'

'Not your pecker which I'm sure is quite------well your toy boy would know all about that I'm sure'

'I've no idea----------'Richard stammered.

'Oh come on now I'm sure you have some little idea what I'm getting at Richard. Had you another little tryst with your toy boy last night, is that where you're coming from now, one more riding session before the little wife returns?'

The blood drained from Richard's face and he said,
'You wouldn't, you wouldn't ------'

Joyce then looked at her watch and said, 'My goodness but we are early. Fancy a cup of coffee and a chat before we hit the office Richard? Let's have a little chat about an upcoming equestrian event I'm organizing, a riding session, between us, me and you that is, and the opportunity to save your reputation as the man most desired as a riding partner by all the girls in the office. And then by arriving in together late, very late, give the gossiping class something to talk about. Which I will ever so discretely be able to vouch for, and maintain the reputation of the ride of the office-----and the man I saw in a compromising position with his toy boy last Saturday night in Albert Walk'

Francie

Francie Shannon was a vagrant almost all his life. He was living on the streets since he was twelve, that was when his alcohol addicted mother died and he ran away from the institution he was committed to by the state authorities who could not be bothered searching for him when he went missing.

After all there were lots of other Francie's in the system and who was going to miss one. He had no idea who his father was, and all his mother ever said about him when he asked was that he had died before Francie was born. Whoever he was he wished he had not died before he had known him and that they could have all lived together as a normal happy family. That was Francie's fondest wish to be part of a normal loving family.

He was now in his thirties and after a short hiatus when he thought his luck had changed he was back on the streets again. Only this time it was worse than before because now he had had a taste of what normal living was like and he had lost that and felt he would never get that chance for happiness again.

For the past four years home for Francie had been a disused old amusement arcade in a laneway in Bray, in Albert Walk. Francie was born on the streets and almost all his memories were of street life, and until his luck temporally changed for a while there was nothing else in his life to connect him with a normal upbringing like most of the people who passed him in the lane or on the prom where he walked most days, nothing except the cheap neck locket with a picture of his mother he carried with him at all times.

The locket was broken, there was only one side of what he suspected had been a two picture locket on the chain, the side with his mother's face, the other part was missing. Who he often wondered was the other picture of. But broken or not it was his most prized possession, it was his only possession. The face of his mother smiled at him from that locket on what must have been one of her rare happy days. All that was visible to him was the face of a young girl with what he knew was blond hair and blue eyes, but she was smiling and she was beautiful then, not like his later memories of her as she succumbed to the scourge of alcohol that emaciated her body and tormented her mind.

In so far as she could be she was a good mother to Francie but too often she was consumed with the need to feed her habit and that's when Francie was confronted with his mother being abused by a succession of men.

They lived rough for a while and then his mother formed a relationship with a man who allowed them to live in the basement of a house he owned near Mountjoy Square in the city. But his mother had to pay for that privilege with her body, to the man and to his friends whom he forced her to have sex with. That was the pattern of Francie's young life, a less than happy childhood, occasionally attending school, and seeing his mother being abused by men. His mother's condition got gradually worse due to her consumption of alcohol, in an effort no doubt to numb the pain of her futile existence, and the man who had let them stay in the basement, when he and his friends no longer found having sex with his mother a pleasing experience evicted them from the basement flat.

They would he had no doubt be replaced by some other poor girl who would become their plaything until she too was worn out. His mother did not last long after that and she was taken from the open hall way of an abandoned tenement house they were sheltering in one night and brought to St James's hospital while he was sent to a home for wayward kids. Two or three days later a social worker told him his mother was dead and he was to be transferred to an institution to await being placed in a foster home. It was the social worker who gave him the locket he now treasured, saying,
'This is all she had on her, I suppose you should have it'

After her death Francie was placed in an institution for the children of alcoholics, both dead and alive and after a few days he decided that the life he had spent on the streets would be better than what was on offer there and so one rainy evening when the wardens, that's what he called them, were otherwise engaged Francie absconded.

He hid out in abandoned houses and laneways for a while and fed himself by nicking cakes and chocolate from the new open shelved self service stores and eating the left over fruit he found in Moore Street at night after the dealers had gone home and he scarpered whenever he saw a Garda but after a while he realized that no one was looking for him, he was expendable.

And so the years passed and Francie grew into his teenage year's becoming a well known figure amongst his peers on the streets of Dublin. He was a good looking lad, tall and well built despite his restricted diet, and he had inherited his mother's blond hair and blue eyes and he had, had he wanted it, his pick of the street women, and it must be said, the men, some of whom propositioned Francie with offers they thought he could not refuse.

That life though was not for Francie. He started visiting the libraries and museums of the city, at first to get in out of the cold but he became fascinated by what was on exhibition and although his reading ability was limited he often picked up a book and tried with his limited capacity for words to comprehend what was written on the page. That was how he passed his teenage years and it helped keep him out of major trouble with the law. He preferred that way of life to becoming involved in the new scourge of drugs and alcohol that he could see was the downfall of many of his compatriots.

It was in a library Dolores noticed him. How could she not, he did stand out with his height, he was over six feet tall, his good physique, his overall good looks and his unkempt blond hair and piercing blue eyes, and she suspected that he was a street person by his appearance and watched him carefully in case he would steal a book. He never did, but he kept coming back and after a few weeks of watching him, and now she was watching him not because she thought he would steal a book but because he was, well he was pleasant on the eye.

One day as Francie was leafing through the pages of Joyce's 'Dubliner's' Dolores decided to speak to him.

'Hello' she said as Francie's finger was tracing out a word on the page,

'Are you fond of Joyce?'

Francie was startled and quickly closed the book and looking up at the woman standing over him asked,

'Joyce? Joyce who? I don't know anyone called Joyce'

Dolores smiled and pointed to the cover of the book that was now face up on the table. Francie still did not get it and stood up to leave and then Dolores realized that just maybe he was not being humorous or funny.

'No don't go, I'm sorry if I interrupted you. It's just that I'm the librarian and I've noticed you spend a lot of time here and I was wondering if you would care to join one of our book clubs, we have clubs for all tastes, and seeing you reading 'Dubliner's' well I just thought you were a student of James Joyce'

'Oh' Francie said 'James Joyce? Did he write this?'

Dolores then realized that despite Francie's, well 'sexy' appearance he was innocent and not well educated.

'Yes, yes he did, as well as other books--------he was one of Irelands best and most famous writers'

Francie did not say anything in reply to what the librarian had said but just stood looking fascinated at the lady in front of him who had spoken to him with words that did not threaten or abuse him. The first time anyone with---well no respectable lady had ever spoken to him before and this lady, well she was beautiful he realized and as he looked at her he began to blush--------- in case she could guess what he was thinking.

She was very attractive and his eyes were attracted to her bosom. He could see her cleavage being pressed together by the rather low necked dress she was wearing and it began to excite him. He had never had full sex with anyone and as he looked at the lady in front of him he wondered what it would be like with her. Oh sure some of the street girls had let him, well, they had put his hand on their breast's and between their legs when they were drunk or had attempted to touch him on his private parts in the hope that they could get him excited and have sex with him, but he had never become aroused or excited by them and had never wanted to do anything with them and their breast were not like this lady's, they were flaccid and scrawny not attractive and sexy like the lady's were.

He felt the heat of his face was evident to see and a stirring started in his loose trouser bottoms because of what he was thinking and he embarrassingly fumbled to pick up the book from the table and held it in front of his crotch. Dolores noticed his eyes on her bosom and his action with the book, and as she glanced down to where he was holding the book she could see what he was trying to hide and she then began to have a strange sensation overcome her and she began to blush too as she diverted her eyes from his crotch and tried to cast aside what she was thinking.

'Well I'll let you get back to your reading, Mr-----' she said and in a somewhat flustered and confused state hurried back to her desk.

They were both disoriented by the experience, and the strength of the physical attraction they both felt. Francie in a somewhat pleasant and excited way that an attractive lady would talk to him like that, and despite the embarrassment he had felt when he became aroused he liked the experience. Her presence had succeeded in arousing him in a way no one had ever done before and he sat down until the sense of excitement passed. He had never been aroused like that by any of the street girls and they had been there for the taking had he wanted any of them and they were younger than the lady, but she was beautiful and he could not stop thinking of her.

And Dolores, well it had been a long time since her last relationship and she did miss the physical intimacies a man in her life brought. But she was extremely embarrassed and surprised by the feelings the encounter with the young man had aroused in her. After all he was----she tried not to let the fact of his station in life defuse the strength of the attraction she felt, he was a very good looking young man. But how she had felt aroused at seeing---this embarrassment came with a sense of sensual pleasure and excitement that had been lacking in her life for quite a while.

But despite her embarrassment she was also very pleased that she could have that kind of effect, which she obviously had, on a younger very attractive man.

Francie remained in the library until closing time and when he was leaving with eyes cast downward he shyly said good night to Dolores as he passed her desk and went out into the night. She in turn said good night to Francie and wondered as she watched him leave, with just a small pang of envy, with whom and where he would spend the night. He went to Burdock's and purchased a Cod and chips and found the concealed doorway in a lane off Grafton Street where he kept his sleeping bag and sat with the sleeping bag over his shoulders and had his meal, all the while thinking of his encounter with the attractive lady in the library and the effect it had on him while Dolores in somewhat more luxurious surroundings was thinking of Francie.

Would he dare to come in again today Dolores was thinking as she sat on the train to town from her home in Bray the next morning. Despite her disturbing experience yesterday she was just a little bit exhilarated by it all and the sensual effect it had on her. Nothing remotely like it had happened to her in a very long time. And despite what she now knew Francie to be she hoped he would come back today.

Francie was faced with a dilemma, he had not noticed Dolores before yesterday because when he entered and left the library he had done so with his head down in case he was stopped and told it was off limits to him, like a lot of other places. But all that had changed now, the lady had spoken to him, and had even invited him to join a club. Still he had almost made a fool of himself and he hoped the lady had not noticed-----well it was embarrassing how he could not control his emotions and he debated with himself as to whether he should show his face there again.

Dolores walked the short distance from the train station to the library all the while thinking of Francie and whether she would ever see him again. After yesterday's incident and Francie's reaction to her display of cleavage she had been undecided what to wear today in case, well in case he came in again. She had a good figure and liked to---- not flaunt it exactly but she was a sensual woman and saw no reason not to be proud of what she had and so decided to wear a dress somewhat similar to the one she had worn yesterday, one with a low neckline that emphasised her bosom. If he keeps coming to the library he will just have to get used to seeing some cleavage exposed she decided as she dressed and admired the result in the mirror.

At three o'clock in the afternoon, just when Dolores had thought Francie was not going to come today he scurried in as usual with his head down and proceeded to the shelves and seemed to just grab a book at random and went to a table and began to read. She kept her eyes on him for a while and suddenly noticed what she had not noticed before, he read with his finger going from word to word, he could not read, or at least could not read well.

At six o'clock Francie replaced the book on the shelf and pulled his coat up around his ears and as he was passing her desk, not saying goodnight as he had last night, Dolores called,

'Good Night Mr.----'

Francie stopped and turned towards Dolores and replied, 'Good Night Miss-----'

'Dowling' Dolores replied with a smile, 'Dolores Dowling'

Francie swallowed hard and walked back to the desk and looked at Dolores and as their eyes met and each looked into the window of the others soul and could see the longing there that each of them was eager to satisfy he said, 'Francie Shannon'

That was a long time ago and a lot had happened to Francie since that day. Against all the odds Francie, the twenty one year old vagrant and Dolores the thirty one year old librarian formed a relationship and in time he moved in with her to her home in Bray. She taught him to read and helped get him a job in the library service, as a janitor in another library, and for a while things were going well for the pair.

Then Dolores contracted cancer and in two months was dead. Dolores's rented accommodation was too expensive for Francie to keep paying on a janitor's wage so after a short time he fell into arrears with the rent and he was evicted from the house he had found so much happiness in for a short time.

It proved to be too much for Francie. After being picked up off the floor by Dolores and enjoying the intimacies of a loving relationship and now losing it all again,-----Francie just could not cope with the sadness and despondency he now felt. Dolores had provided him with security and stability, just as his mother had in her way, but now that was gone and his new lonely situation was too much for him to handle.

For a while after the eviction he lived in a hostel but that environment only contributed to the collapse of his mental health and he started missing days at work and eventually lost his job which resulted in him not being able to afford the cost of the hostel and he ended up on the streets again.

He was back in the city now and started to congregate with his old cohorts, with those few of them who were still alive that is, and he, like his mother before him turned to drink to ease his pain.

He was still only in his late twenties and still had a good physique and this attribute is what caused some men to pay him the money he needed for drink to be allowed abuse his body and torture his mind. Francie was disgusted by this weakness in his character and hated succumbing to the need for drink to do the things he did and allowed be done to him and contemplated suicide as a means of escaping his wretched existence. It was at this point during a brief period of sobriety that he realized he had to make a change to his life and as he recollected the happy times he had spent with Dolores in Bray he decided that is where he would go to escape the desolation of the city.

That was four years ago and after spending some time in various locations including in the little sun shelters on the prom he was now firmly ensconced in the basement of a disused old amusement arcade on Albert Walk. It was quiet there and few knew he was there and that suited him.

Few if any ventured down the laneway now, not like years ago when Albert Walk was almost a main thoroughfare to the beach from the train station and the day trippers packed it from end to end, but those days were long over and Francie was secure in his spartan accommodation.

On fine days Francie would walk along the prom and if he had the money have a coffee in 'The Coffee Dock' the restaurant that had been established in the old boat house near Bray Head. He kept himself clean and tidy by washing in the public toilets and the ladies in the coffee shop always treated him with respect because they remembered when he and Dolores used to stop by and have coffee there.

The days he could just about tolerate but the nights were hard. That's when the memories came to life and he had trouble discerning what was real, and what was his imagination.

Through all his trials and tribulations he had somehow managed to keep safe the broken locket left to him by his mother and he turned to it for comfort when things got too much for him. One night after a particularly tough lonely day walking around Bray with not a cent in his pocket he returned to his abode in the basement of the old arcade and in frustration began pulling the place apart looking to see if there might be some old coins somewhere about the place that had been hidden by time that would enable him to buy a cup of tea or coffee.

As he searched in the quickly descending darkness his fingers felt something round under a broken skirting board and he latched onto it and pulled it out thinking it might be a coin of some description. He held the disc in his hand and rubbed the accumulated dust of many years from it and before his startled eyes a young man's smiling face stared back at him.

In amazement he looked at the picture and then he held the newly found disc to his mother's broken locket and it was a perfect fit to the broken locket, the other half of a love locket showing the smiling faces of two young lovers.

That was the day she was happy he thought, that was the day she had a reason to smile. Now he knew who his father was. That may even have been the day he was conceived he thought to himself, the day they were a happy family.

Holding the now complete again locket tightly in his hand he lay down on the old mattress that was his bed in the basement of the old amusement arcade and as the distant sound of a busker quietly crooning a lullaby in the lane outside soothed his mind he died a happy man.

Rosie and Sally's First Holiday

Rosie and Sally were lifelong friends and had lived in the same crumbling tenement in the city until it was condemned and they and their families were moved to the new corporation estate in Cabra and now lived in spanking new houses with a garden, inside toilet and a bath.

When they left the girls primary school in Wellington Street at age fourteen they both began working in a soap factory in the centre of Dublin and their life as young adults began. They were an adventurous pair especially Rosie, who was the more outgoing of the pair and was always to the forefront of their adventures and because her body developed faster than Sally's was very popular with the boys, and this made Sally annoyed at times as she wanted to monopolize her attention. Sally was not too fussed about getting attention from boys although some did court her attention but as long as she could have Rosie as a companion she was happy.

They often went to the cinema together and they were mesmerized by the Technicolor travelogues they saw there. And seeing scenes of faraway sunny places made them wish they could some day visit those places too. They so wished they could visit those resorts and for a few weeks at least bask in the sunshine that was so lacking in Ireland.

As they grew into their teenage years and now felt themselves to be independent young women and had been earning good money in the soap factory for three years Sally suggested one day that they should go on a holiday together and so they decided to go on a holiday when the factory closed in the summer. They were not so adventurous though that they would go foreign, not for the first time anyway, but decided that for their first ever holiday they would go to Bray.

They were seventeen years of age now and had never been on a holiday before in their lives so they decided to start local and then, next year who knows where they would go. When August came around and it was time to pack their cases the excitement was palpable as they crammed their cardboard suitcases with almost all the clothes they possessed and prepared for a week of -------well they did not know what they would do when they were out of sight and control of their parents, after all they had heard that Bray could be a wild place in the summer, what with all the Northern Irish boys and even English and Scottish lads there, why it might even be as good as going foreign Rosie had said.

They knew that they would be skipping saying the Rosary and going to mass that week, that was for sure, after all there might be Protestant boys there and they would not want that, religion that is, to get in the way of a bit of romance. They would be staying in lodgings in Albert Walk, wherever that was, for their week in Bray. This had all been arranged for them by the factory manager, Mr Layfield, when they told him that they were thinking of taking a holiday when the factory closed, as it did every year for the first two weeks of August.

'You can't beat Bray' he had said 'sure you have everything you could want on a holiday there, amusement arcades, cafe's, a lovely prom, the sea, bingo halls and sure there's even a cinema and plenty of shops. And if you're not afraid of heights sure they even have a chair lift up to Bray Head. Sure you may as well be in Switzerland or some such place, it's like heaven on that chair lift so it is as it carries you up the Head' he had eulogized. Rosie and Sally were won over by his description and as they had never been outside Dublin before sure it was bound to be exciting and decided that exotic Bray was to be the destination of their very first holiday on their own, their very first holiday ever. They discussed their holiday for weeks every lunch hour with Mr Layfield and it was he who told them of the lodging house he and his wife Mabel stayed in the first time they went to Bray. And when he spoke of it he seemed to, well he seemed for some reason or other to get all misty eyed and a big smile spread across his face as if he was thinking of something very pleasant. Then he snapped out of it and said it was very reasonable and it held good memories for him and if it was up to him he would still be staying there when he went to Bray, but in those days he was just a factory hand and now he was the factory manager so Mabel had insisted that the lodgings they choose should reflect his position in society, so now they stayed in a premises on the prom, a hotel, 'The Esplanade' which was nearer the Head and more expensive but was frequented by----by a better class of guest he said with not a hint of embarrassment or shame in his voice. But still he said he could recommend the guest house on Albert Walk unreservedly because it held very good memories for him and Mabel.

Layfield wrote to the lodgings on behalf of the girls and arranged for the letting and so all there was to do then was to wait for August to come around.

The girls had never been to Bray although it was only a short train journey from Dublin but the fact that it had County Wicklow attached to its name gave the impression it was a foreign country and inaccessible to natives of Dublin and so their experience of seaside holidays consisted of day trips to Sandymount or Dollymount, even Howth it seemed was too exotic to venture to.

On the Friday they finished work they were so excited and after saying good bye to all their workmates, as if they were heading on an expedition to wildest Africa or somewhere, they cycled home to their new corporation houses in Cabra and began putting the finishing touches to their packing and preparing for their holiday odyssey. They, like most of the girls in the factory were in a chemist club, that is they paid a few pence a week into a fund and each week it was some girls turn to draw the money she had paid over the previous ten or twenty weeks and redeem it for cosmetics in the chemist that organized the scheme. It was Rosie's turn this week and because they were going on holiday's she had agreed to share her fund with Sally, Sally when it was her turn to collect would then share it with Rosie. So after tea they had agreed to meet and before the chemist closed, luckily it was Friday and the chemist remained open late on Friday, they hurried down to Dargan's on Berkley Road and picked the lipstick, mascara, eye liner, face powder and a few other cosmetics to beautify themselves for their holiday.

All was now ready, and in a state of heightened anticipation they set the time to meet at nine thirty to get the bus into town and then the eleven o'clock train from Amiens Street station.

All went well until they reached the station and as it was a holiday weekend the station was packed and they had never been in a train station before so they had no idea what to do or where to go.

They had somehow thought that it would be like getting a bus, just get on the train and pay the conductor and wait till your stop was called, but there were seven platforms in the station and a train on each one. It confused the hell out of them. They stood with their cases in their hands in a state of total bewilderment not knowing what to do or where to go. Then they heard an indistinct sound above their heads and in the midst of the cacophony thought they heard the word Bray, but they could not be sure as they had no idea what was happening. They looked at each other in a state of near panic and Sally shouted to Rosie above the noise,
'Oh Rosie we should not have ventured out of Dublin, this is a terrible place I hope Bray is not like this', to which Rosie replied,
'We're not out of Dublin yet Sally, this is a part of the city no one ever told us about'
'We better ask someone for help or the train will go without us, it's almost ten to eleven' Sally then said.

As the crowds of travellers bustled all around them they saw a man pulling a trolley load of cases and in an act of desperation Rosie stepped forward held her hand up in front of the fast approaching man and said,
'How do we get to the Bray train from here Mister'

The 'Mister' who was only a little older than the girls stopped in his tracks when he saw the two good looking girls in a state of distress and smiled at them and said,
'And on behalf of CIE how can I help you young ladies today?' and made a mock bow in front of them.

'How do we get to the Bray train?' Rosie repeated.

'The Bray train is it, and do you have tickets for the Bray train?' he asked them being serious and officious now in an effort to impress the girls.

'Tickets?' Sally replied confused by his question.

'Yes you'll need tickets to get on the train' the young man replied in a self important and officious manner.

'I, we,----- we thought we paid the conductor when we got on' Rosie then said equally as confused as Sally.

'Ah girls sure you're not on the Crumlin bus now, this is the modern way to travel' he replied and laughed at the girl's dilemma.   'Please mister' Sally then said 'where do we get the tickets?'
'You should have got them from the ticket kiosk at the top of the stairs before you came to the platform, but there's a big queue there now and the Bray train leaves in two minutes so it does' he replied pressing home his advantage to impress the girls

'Oh God what will we do at all Rosie?' Sally then said as if this was the most distressing dilemma they would ever encounter in their lives and looked at Rosie with a look of desperation on her face.

'I'm never going on holidays again so I'm not' Rosie replied, 'it's too dangerous'
'So it's holidays your on is it, and you're going to Bray? You're a saucy pair and no doubt, what age are you, sixteen? And going on holidays on your own to Bray?'
Then with a mischievous twinkle in his eyes,
'Tell us this now girls where abouts in Bray are you staying?' the trolley puller asked and winked at the girls.

'We're seventeen, going on eighteen and we're not from Crumlin. If you must know we're from Cabra and it's no business of yours where we're staying in Bray' Rosie replied highly indignant at his attitude.
The young man smiled and with a little chuckle said,
'Come on so or you'll miss your train. The Bray train leaves in a minute,------ but it's the one just behind you so I'll vouch for your honesty to get the tickets when you get to Bray so get into that carriage and enjoy your holiday'

And as Rosie and Sally turned around to look at the train which was standing on the tracks not more than a few yards from them a loud whistling noise sounded and they stepped forward and the young man opened the carriage door and helped the girls into an already almost full carriage. They were no sooner on than the engineer began working up a head of steam and the train began pulling out of the station. As it was slowly exiting the station the young man with the trolley was keeping pace with it and before the train gathered speed and moved away he called out to the girl's.

'Don't forget to bring me back a stick of rock, I'll be watching out for you next week'

'Mr Layfield said Albert Walk was only a short distance from the station and we'll have no trouble finding it, I hope he's right. God that was awful confusion in the station, I don't want anything like that to happen again' Sally said as the train huffed and puffed its way to Bray and they were mesmerized by the scenery along the way especially when the train reached where they could see the coast and when they reached Dalkey and entered the tunnel that leads to Killiney they actually shrieked with delight as the train emerged from the darkness of the tunnel to the spectacular view of Killiney Bay.

'Oh Sally this is magnificent, it's like something you'd see at the pictures so it is, are we still in Ireland at all?'

'Are you still not going to go on holidays again Rosie?'

Sally asked an enraptured Rosie as she stood with her head half way out the window spellbound looking at the passing beauty of the blue sea and the sailing boats in the water and the Wicklow Mountains and Bray Head in the distance.

'Only to Bray Sally' Rosie replied with a smile on her face.

Presently they reached Bray Station and the steam train exhausted its last few puffs of smoke and with a long loud whistle announced its arrival to the inhabitants of the town. As requested by the man in Amiens Street station Sally and Rosie made straight to the ticket office and told the ticket seller what had happened in Amiens street and offered to pay the fare but the good weather must have softened his cough and he just waved them off saying,

'I've enough trouble trying to get used to all these newfangled gadgets s and rules being introduced by CIE as it is to be bothered getting tangled up in selling tickets for journeys already completed. Just arrive in enough time to buy your tickets before you start your journey in future like two good girls will you'

And as he seemed like a nice man after letting them off with the fare the girls asked him for directions to Albert Walk.

'Just walk out of the station, turn to your left and diagonally across from you is Albert Walk. There's a stone marker on the corner, you can't miss it, even if you wanted to, and with the god awful noise that bloody busker is making over there maybe you should give it a miss'

So after all the hassle of the morning they were at last on holiday and ready to see what Bray had to offer. They walked the short distance from the station to the laneway a few yards to their left as the ticket seller had indicated and as they approached they could hear the sounds of the busker the ticket seller in the station had been complaining of and to their young ears he did not sound that bad at all.

He was singing 'The Tennessee Waltz' and playing a guitar as he sang. That song had been a big hit for Patti Page and Rosie and Sally together with the other girls in the factory had often sung it as they worked on the conveyor belt to while away the monotony and they smiled at the man as they passed and felt guilty that they had not put a few pennies in the hat he had on the ground, but promised to themselves that they would when they settled in, they were sure he would be there then.

The narrow lane way was packed with people walking up and down the artery eating ice cream cones and candy floss. It was a hive of activity and noise. There were shops of every description, ice cream parlours, amusement arcades, tea rooms, novelty stores, chippers and even notices advertising fortune tellers. They had never seen anything like it before, except at the pictures.

No 4 Albert Walk was a two story house with a small garden set a little way back from the main walkway and this was where Sally and Rosie's lodgings were situated. When they saw how busy the laneway was they were glad that they were just that little way back from all the activity.

They knocked on the door which was quickly opened by an elderly man dressed all in black. They each stood looking at each other and then the man asked them,
'Yes, what can I do for you?'
'We're booked in for the week' Rosie replied to which the man said,
'I'm sorry I already have a booking in the name of a Mr Layfield'
'That's us' Sally chimed in, 'Mr Layfield booked it for us'

'Who are you and what do you want?' The man then asked and was about to shut the door without receiving an answer when Rosie said,

'Mr-----Mr Layfield is our boss and he booked us in here for a week's holiday'

The man then stopped his attempt to close the door and looking at the two girls said,

'There's been a mistake, I don't -----I don't take women lodgers in here I have my reputation to think of. You'll have to go someplace else'

'But we, ----we don't know where to go, we don't know Bray, we're from Dublin, from Cabra and we have nowhere else to go' the girls protested. The man continued to look at them and then he sighed and said,

'Oh I suppose if you're booked in I'll have to let you stay, I would not want to be responsible for turning two young girls out on the streets of Bray on a holiday weekend'

And then he sighed again and said to himself as if the girls were not there, 'What is this country coming to at all, young girls holidaying on their own, what kind of parents have they got at all?'

He then looked directly at Rosie and Sally and said in a stern almost fatherly way,

'I expect you to keep regular hours while you are here and on no account are you to bring boys back to this house. In fact don't bring anyone back. Do you hear me? Any alcohol found on the premises will be destroyed. By me, personally. Do you understand? And no smoking in bed mind. And no loud noise'

Rosie and Sally looked at each other as the noise of the music being played in the background was nearly deafening them and after a moments silence both of them replied, 'Yes Mister'

'Good', he replied, 'I'll be back next week to check you out, and to check the house. Enjoy your holiday in Bray'

And with that he picked up his folded umbrella and put on his hat and left Sally and Rosie standing with their mouths open as he walked out and with a loud bang closed the door.

The two girls were, to quote a well know song, bewitched, bothered and bewildered by the sequence of events that had happened since they left the sanctuary of their homes this morning and if they had had any drink and if they had drank they would at that moment have gulped down a large strong whiskey to relieve the tension they felt and to bring them back to their senses.

But all they had was the means of making a cup of tea and this they did in almost complete silence, because each of them was trying in their minds to comprehend the events of the day. The holiday had not started the way they had expected but after the tea party they began to relax a bit and decided the best thing to do was refresh themselves and put on clean fresh clothes and go out into the bright lights of Bray and begin their holiday and try to forget all that had happened up to this, this was the start of their holiday and they were going to enjoy it, come what may.

After the drabness of a corporation housing estate Bray seafront was a revelation. The weather was still warm and the women were promenading about in summer dresses and the men in trousers and open necked white shirts. For their parts Rosie and Sally were in summer dresses, Rosie in a multi coloured floral design and Sally in a pale blue dress with white facings with cardigans around their shoulders and each of them were in fashionable pump type walking shoes, Rosie's plain white and Sally's white with a cherry red heel and toe.

It was a Saturday night and everywhere was open and there was music to be heard coming from the cafe's and the carnival that was on the grass apron of the prom. They had walked down to the seafront and were hanging over the railings looking at the white waves gently disturbing the stones on the pebbly beach and feeling as free as they had ever felt in their young lives.

'Let's have a go on the bumpers' Rosie said as the holiday atmosphere began to take a hold of them and the earlier events began to fade and they walked across to where the amusements were situated.

They waited until the cars stopped and then they ran to secure a car for themselves for the next go. Rosie as usual was first to reach an empty car and took the wheel and when the ride commenced she expertly steered the car away from a car with two boys in it who were about to crash into them and laughed as the boys failed to hit them.

They drove away from the rest of the cars and then realized that the two boys were in hot pursuit again and as they again tried to hit them Rosie maneuvered the car to her left and the boys car hit the edge of the circuit and the two boys bounced forward with the force of the impact.

As Rosie drove away laughing from the embarrassed boys the rage was palpable on the boys faces and in a fit of anger they attempted to ram the girls car one more time but the man in charge of the bumpers had been watching them and before they could ram the car he cut the power and the boys car stopped inches from the girls car and before they could react the bumper man ran and pulled the boys from the car and put them out of the bumper arena.

They were livid and as they stood glaring at Rosie and Sally the man put on the power again and Rosie and Sally continued with their ride. They stayed in the car for a second trip and by the time that was finished the two boys were gone and Sally and Rosie stayed in the carnival compound and partook of rides on the big wheel, the chair-a-planes and the swinging boats before they continued their walk along the prom and near the Bray Head Hotel they bought fish and chips from a small vendors hut and sat and listened to the sea as they ate their supper.

Then they noticed the Tudor style black and white facing Bray Head Hotel was all lit up and warm looking and as an evening chill descended on Bray they wondered if they could dare to go in. They were only seventeen and did not drink nor frequent pubs, but the way they had dolled themselves up they were sure they could pass for girls of twenty and so they plucked up the courage and with an air of fake confidence sauntered over to the hotel and walked in.

Nobody said anything to them so they sat at a table near the window in the red velvet upholstered lounge and when the waitress came to them Rosie asked for two dressed orange drinks, which were served without question. They sat luxuriating in the plush red upholstered chairs observing all around them and smiling to themselves that they were so sophisticated to be on holidays and feeling so grown up. Before they left the hotel and after having another round of dressed orange drinks in fancy glasses Rosie had to go to the toilet and as she looked about her to see where the toilets were a handsome young man approached her and asked if he could be of assistance, he was an assistant manager of the hotel and he accompanied her to the toilets and held the door open for her as she entered. She was enamoured by the attention and thanked him with a smile.

Their first day in Bray had been nothing if not eventful and after drinking the orange juice in the lounge of the Bray Head Hotel they walked arm in arm back to their lodgings tired but elated that they had successfully negotiated the first day of their first holiday on their own in Bray and after a hot cup of tea made in the kitchen of their lodgings they went upstairs to their bedroom and went to bed in a large double bed and studiously avoided touching each other as they slept.

They didn't get up for mass the next morning which was a Sunday but they didn't care and felt no guilt, they were on their holidays and to them that was good enough reason not to do the things they always did.

When at about twelve o'clock Rosie called to Sally and asked if she wanted a cup of tea Sally pulled the sheet from her head and smiled at her and said,
'I was hoping you would get up first because I always wanted someone to bring me my breakfast in bed'
'I said a cup of tea not breakfast, if you want that you can go to one of the tea rooms on The Walk'
As she said this she threw the covers from her side of the bed off her and got up and walked across the room.

She was wearing a baby doll top and a pair of matching frilly knickers and as she stood at the door Sally looked at her and realized that although they had been friends all their lives this was the first time they had ever shared a bedroom or seen each other,----well seen what was under the clothes they wore.

Though she had to admit to herself that she had often fantasized about Rosie and what she would look like without clothes. Her body was much more developed than hers was, she knew that because of the way she filled tops and sweaters, and this was one of the reasons Sally fantasized about her. She looked so much more mature than she did.

And looking at Rosie in her baby doll pyjamas, which she had not noticed last night because they undressed and put on their night wear in the dark, she could see that womanly development close up and wondered if there was a chance that Rosie might have similar feelings for her. Sally called to Rosie intending to say thanks for getting up to make the tea but when Rosie turned to face her she could see the full extent of the maturity of her body and she was speechless.

She was only seventeen, the same age as she was but her bust was as developed as any she had ever seen, certainly more developed than hers, even more than some of those film stars in the Hollywood film magazines that she liked looking at she thought.

'What? What else do you want besides tea? Do you want a biscuit, there's some in a tin I seen in the kitchen' Rosie replied as Sally stared at her.

'What's wrong, why are you staring like that?' Rosie asked and Sally replied wistfully,

'My God but you're beautiful Rosie'

Rosie laughed and said,

'What's got into you, sure we girls are all the same we all have the same bits and pieces so we have'

'Your breast, it's so big, so much fuller and bigger than mine'

'Oh the boy bait' Rosie replied smiling and held her boobs in her hands, 'I hadn't noticed' she laughed, 'the boys have though'

Sally continuing to stare at Rosie replied more seriously,

'This is the first time we've ever seen each other without our cloths on and you're so beautiful Rosie'

'Yea well that can't be helped I suppose. And seeing as we're in the same bedroom getting dressed and our bodies are on show well------sure we are bound to see each other I suppose' Rosie replied nonchalantly.

Sally then got out of bed and walked towards Rosie
and as she did she removed her long linen nightdress which
was up to her neck and down to her ankles exposing her
smaller though still perky and attractive breast hoping the
sight of her nakedness would provoke some reaction in Rosie
but as there was none and Rosie appeared to take little notice
of her she said,
'I wish I had breast's like yours Rosie, instead of----'
'Sally' Rosie said, 'I think you have a lovely body. I love
your breasts, they're so pert and firm, they suit your slim
body'
Sally smiled and cupped her small firm breasts in her
hands and as she did so said,
'God Rosie imagine if anyone seen us like this they'd think
we were,------- what do you call them, lesbos or something'
'Well I'm not, I like boys, I want to get married some
day and have loads of kids so I do' Rosie replied pointedly to
Sally's remarks.
As Rosie said this she turned away from Sally and
unconcernedly lifted her top above her head and threw it onto
the bed allowing Sally appreciate the full extent of her bust
and began searching in her cardboard case for a bra.
'Have you ever had sex with a boy Rosie' Sally asked as
Rosie, still naked, rummaged in her case.

'Not really, not full sex but I did let Jimmy Buckley, you know the van driver at work, have a feel of my breast one night after a dance in the Kingsway. He had been lurching with me all night and pressing himself against me and when the dance was over he insisted on leaving me home and, well we went into the grotto at Berkley Road church for a ware and his hands were all over me so just to stop him pestering me, because he never stopped asking if he could see my bust, I let him see it and feel it. God you should have seen him when I lifted me bra and took me tits out, it was as if he had got his fondest Christmas wish and I swear Sally he was salivating as he touched me. He was about to put his mouth on it but I wasn't having any of that, if he wanted to be breast fed he should go home to his mother I told him and I whipped them back into me bra and pushed his head away'

'Ah Jasus Rosie' he said, sounding as if a steak dinner had been whipped from under his knife and fork before he had a chance to taste it ' I'd love to get me mouth around them beauties, you have a great pair of tits, will you be me girl friend?'

'I will not I told him, I'm too young to be any ones girl friend, I want to have a good time before I start going steady with anyone'

'With the size of your bust I suppose it would be on any boy's Christmas list to touch it' Sally said and handed Rosie a bra that she picked out of the case.

'God it can get so annoying at times, all some fellahs want is to have a feel. It's as if all you are to them is a pair of tits. And you, have you, has any boy-----'
Rosie asked as she positioned her breasts into the cups of her bra.

'God no Rosie' Sally replied.

'Have you never had sex with anyone Sally'

'No not yet, but I think I'd prefer it with girls'

'How do you know if you've never had sex with a boy?'

'Well I've, I've seen a boy and that big thing that that they----you know the thing between their legs, well that puts me off so it does'

'When and who's did you see?' Rosie asked as she continued dressing.

'Charlie Walker, the fellah who works in the stores in the factory'

'But Charlie's married with kids Sally, how did you see him?'

'Well he was always pestering me when I had to go to the stores for anything and he tried to kiss me one time so I knew I had to do something or he'd never stop pestering me so one day when I had to go to the stores and he was trying to hug me and asking me for a kiss I got very brazen and said that I'd give him a kiss if he'd let me see his-----you know, his willie. He thought I was serious and all his birthdays had come together and he checked that no one was around and then closed the door and we stood in behind some boxes of soap that was stacked against the wall and he pulled his trousers down and took out his thing and held it in his hand for me to see. And I just burst out laughing and when he asked me what I was laughing at, I said between my put on laughs that I had never seen a willie so small in all my life and he nearly had a seizer and could not put it away quick enough and shouted at me to get out of his stores and never come back'

'And was it really that small Sally?' Rosie asked and Sally tried to hold back the tears of laughter as she replied, 'How would I know, but it was the truth. I'd never seen one before in me life so it was the smallest I had ever seen and the biggest I had ever seen as well. I had heard how proud of their mickey's men were so I thought by embarrassing him he would leave me alone, and he did, he never tormented me for a kiss again, in fact he would not look at me after that'

'Jesus Sally that was a terrible thing to do, poor Charlie I bet he never recovered from that. Anyway I've had enough sex talk for one morning, I'm starving so I am, I'd give me virginity for a fry up right now'

When they were both dressed they went out for something to eat and it was a lovely sunny Sunday afternoon and already the Walk was packed with people and all the shops and kiosks were doing a roaring trade. They went into a cafe on the prom and ordered scrambled eggs and chips as well as a pot of tea, and like ladies of leisure had their meal as they scrutinized the parade of holidaymakers promenading along the seafront. When after about an hour of people watching and they felt it was time to go two young men sat at the next table and when Sally and Rosie got up to leave one of the young men stood up and with arms outstretched said, 'Ah Ladies please don't leave now, sure it was the vision of your loveliness sitting there that attracted us to sit here in the first place'
The girls were stopped in their tracks by this remark and Rosie looked at Sally and whispered to her,
'What do you think? I quite fancy the blond one'
Sally was not so keen and indicated that they should go so Rosie smiled at the two men and said,
'Sorry boys but we have an appointment elsewhere'

'Oh how I wish I was that appointment' the blond man replied and reached out and took Rosie's hands in his and in an elaborate mock gesture kissed them both.

Rosie was flattered and amused by his behaviour and replied in a way that she thought would be complementary to his gallant behaviour,

'Perhaps our paths will cross again kind sir, if destiny so decrees'

'Ah a cultured lady, so rare in these barbaric times, so rare and so beautiful' he replied and with that Sally gestured that they should go. When they were back on the prom Rosie asked,

'Why did you not want to stay, they seemed like two nice boys, and fun to be with. I thought that was part of the reason we came to Bray, so we would meet nice young men'

'I'm sorry Rosie, I just did not feel confident, they seemed like they were, ----well above our class. We're just factory girls from Cabra remember and when boys like that discover it, well they just take what they can get and move on to better things'

'My God Sally, I never knew you felt like that, I don't, I'm the equal of anyone and I feel confident in anyone's company'

The rest of the afternoon, although the weather was warm, was rather chilly in the vicinity of Sally and Rosie and unlike the previous night they did not end the day with a drink in The Bray Head Hotel but after a ten minute losing sequence at the slots they went back to their lodgings in Albert Walk.

It was a Sunday night and it was still bright outside but for Sally and Rosie the night was it seemed over. As they sat in the living room of the lodgings and listened to the music and noise outside in the Walk Rosie said,
'There's a dance in the Arcadia tonight, it's early yet, we could still get ready and go, do you want to do that?'
'I don't think so, you go if you like'
'What's wrong with you Sally, we're on our holidays so we are. We're here to enjoy ourselves'
'I'm enjoying myself with you Rosie. I don't need to go to a dance to be mauled by boys to enjoy myself'
'Sally, I'm enjoying myself with you too, but------I thought that you would like-------'
'You have no idea what I'd like Rosie' Sally interjected as Rosie spoke and went and looked out the window.
Rosie considered what Sally had said and thought about it and then said,
'Earlier today, when you said you'd prefer having sex with girls? What exactly did you mean by that Sally? Did you mean me, that you'd------ And this morning when you, when you remarked on the size of my--------my boobs and stood before me naked, what was that about?'

'Do you not know Rosie? Do you really not know?'
Sally asked and reached her hand out to Rosie. Rosie after a
moment of hesitation took her hand and said,
'I'm not like that Sally, I like boys, I like kissing them
and----- I like them kissing and touching me. But I like you
too, but not that way Sally'
'It's alright Rosie, I just thought you knew the way I
felt about you. But then how could you, there are some things
you cannot---------well in this country you are not allowed to
be the person you really are, maybe someday that will change'
Rosie reached out and embraced Sally and as she did
Sally disengaged from her embrace and said,
'No Rosie, no, don't do that, I've seen what I can never have---
--Rosie it's hard enough knowing that you'll never return the
love I feel for you in the way that-----well I hope we can still
be friends,----- can we?'
'Of course we can Sally, the best of friends----for the
rest of our lives. Tell you what, to seal that deal why don't we
go out and be devils and have a drink, a real drink. We know
we can get into the Bray Head Hotel so why not go and have a
nightcap before we hit the sack'
'Are you still going to share a bed with me, knowing
how-----knowing I'm one of them les things?'
'Of course I am Sally, best friends for the rest of our
lives remember' Rosie smiled and kissed Sally on the cheek
and said,
'Come on get ready, we're on holidays remember'

They got ready and headed for the hotel and when they got there they could see that the chairlift was still operating as there was still some brightness in the sky and Sally said,
'Do you know what Rosie, I'd love to have a go on that chairlift before we go into the hotel, will you come with me?' So they walked up the Head to the departure point and were lucky enough to get the last trip of the evening and they were lifted onto the side by side chairs by the attendant and the safety chain was put on and they set out to The Eagles Nest half way up Bray Head.

As the lift approached its destination and was high above the ground Sally turned and looked at Rosie and she opened the safety chain and said,
'Good bye Rosie, I'll always love you-----for the rest of our lives. But knowing I can never have your love in the way I'd want it would be too painful to live with' and before a startled Rosie could react she lurched forward in the chair throwing herself out of the chair and landing head first on the rocks below, shattering her skull and dying instantly.

The Woman Who Played The Slots

Madge Ryan was in her early fifties and had been a widow since she was thirty. Her husband Tommy Ryan had been her childhood sweetheart, the only man she had ever known, but he had died of TB when he was thirty two leaving Madge a childless widow.

Of the ten years of the marriage Tommy had been sick almost nine. He had contracted TB little more than a year after getting married and for all that time Madge had cared for him, cared for him as if he had been her child and not her husband and lover. Consequently she had never known what a normal husband and wife relationship was. And she missed that love she had been deprived of.

She lived in two rooms of a tenement building in Gardner Street in the centre of Dublin and every Sunday all year round no matter the weather she got up and had a breakfast of rashers, eggs and sausages and then after twelve o'clock mass in Gardner Street church got the train to Bray and spent the rest of the day losing her few pounds pension money in an amusement arcade in Albert Walk, near the train station in Bray. She had been doing that for years, possibly as compensation for the love she had missed and to kill a few hours of the weekend before the long lonely week that came around every Monday after her interlude in Bray took over her life again.

In all those years she had been coming to Bray, in all that time she had sat in the train for about an hour waiting to get to Bray, when she reached her destination she never ventured beyond the arcade in the Walk. She had never seen any more of Bray than what she saw that first time she came and took the short walk from the station to Albert Walk. She had never in fact seen the sea nor strolled on the prom nor went near Bray Head.

The first time she came to Bray was many years ago and she came that day with her sister Teresa, but like her husband Tommy Teresa had also passed away but Madge continued to make the weekly pilgrimage to the shrine of the one armed bandits.

That first time she came to Bray and the reason she only ventured as far as Albert Walk was because there was a downpour when they got off the train and they ran to the nearest place of shelter they could find, which happened to be the small amusement arcade in Albert Walk. She won a few bob that day and so was encouraged to come back to the same arcade the next time she came to Bray, and the next time and the next time and ever since then she had been coming to the same place.

Another reason she did not venture any further was because that first time there had been a busker playing outside in the lane, despite the downpour, and he smiled at her as she and Teresa ran passed him and his smile was so warm and--- he even winked at her and despite her being a widow she liked that, it made her feel like a real woman again after all the years she had been a nurse to Tommy. Nobody apart from her late husband Tommy had ever smiled at her in that way and she could hear his singing as she played the slots and she liked his voice. And he was there every time she came to Bray and he always smiled at her when she passed and she had begun to believe that he sang for her and for her alone when she played the slots.

If, as sometimes she did, win a few bob, she always made sure to throw a few coins into his hat when she was leaving to get the last train back to the city. But despite all that they had never exchanged a word between each other, her and the busker. In all the years she had been coming to Bray the only communication that passed between them was a smile and the songs the busker sang.

She did feel though that over the years they had established some form of silent communication but she could not explain what that was. Sometimes when she was losing too much, more than she could afford to lose, she would get a strong notion that it was time to go and sometimes when she had accumulated a cup full of coins in the container she was supplied with to hold her money she would get the same strong notion that it was time to cash in her winnings and go home. These thought intrusions she somewhat irrationally attributed to the busker because as she left the arcade on those occasions she noticed the busker, if she had won always seemed to be playing and singing a happy song and if she had lost he invariably was looking sad and the song he was singing was also of a sad type.

This silent relationship had gone on for years until one sunny summer Sunday evening when fortune had not been kind to her in the arcade and earlier, much earlier than was usual her money had run out and she was feeling very low and she decided to leave. There was nothing for it but to vacate her stool to some other lonely widow and get an earlier than usual train home. She sighed a sigh of disappointment as the last losing combination of symbols appeared on the window of the slot machine and she began stepping off the stool.

'This must be yours, it was at the foot of the stool' a voice said and as Madge turned to see who was speaking to her she got the surprise of her life. It was the busker and he was holding a shining six penny piece in his hand and offering it to her.
'It's not -----it's not------' She stammered in surprise.
'Go on take it, it must have fallen from your pocket' he said and put the coin down in front of her. She was speechless and did not know what to say.
'It might bring you luck' he said, 'it seems like you have not been having much of that recently' he smiled.
Then Madge composed herself somewhat and taking the coin from the ledge in front of the slot machine said, 'I'll — I'll get change at the kiosk and try my luck a few more times so then'
'No, no don't do that. Put the six pence in'

'But that's more than I usually play, I only ever play with a penny at a time'

'Go for the big one this time Madge' the busker said and smiled at her.

'Madge, he called me Madge, how did he know my name was Madge' Madge thought as she held the coin in her hand and looking at the busker as he indicated that she should play the machine turned and inserted the coin into the recessed place for sixpenny pieces on top of the slot machine and gently pulled the handle.

The three barrels of the machine started to whirr and the numbers and the other symbols on the barrels became an indistinct blur as they raced around in front of her. Round and round the barrels went, seemingly endlessly this time as she, with the busker standing behind her watched and she said, 'You must get a longer spin for six pence' as the barrels showed no sign of stopping.

Then, as her eyes began to get blurred looking at the spinning barrels one suddenly stopped. A golden star appeared in the glass panel. Then seconds later a second golden star appeared and as Madge turned and looked at the busker in excited anticipation he smiled at her and indicated that she should look at the slot.

She turned and to her absolute delight the third golden star fell into place and the barrels stopped spinning. She had won the jackpot. She clasped her hands to her mouth to stifle the sound of joy that was making its way from her throat and as she did the busker said,

'I'll get Willie to change them coins to notes for you and then we'll go and have a cup of tea and a cake'

Ten crisp new pound notes were placed in Madge's hand and with the busker holding her elbow and directing her out of the arcade the two of them, the busker with his guitar on his shoulder and Madge in a trance walked down Albert Walk together as if they had been companions all their lives and at the corner turned left onto Albert Avenue and for the first time since she had been coming to Bray Madge Ryan saw the sea and it looked magical as the white foam of the waves raced towards the pebbles on the foreshore. The busker pointed out Bray Head to Madge and she could see, far up on the top of the mountain the cross that dominated the skyline, and the minute shapes of the people who had climbed all the way up. She could also see the chairlift carrying people up the side of the Head and hear the shrikes of joy of the young people on the carnival rides as they enjoyed all that Bray had to offer. She even had an ice cream cone as they walked and then stood listening for a while to the colourfully suited band that was playing popular airs in the Victorian Bandstand on the prom and on the buskers invitation went with him for a sherry to the red bricked hotel with the three pointed cone shaped towers across from the beach. They took in all the other sights of Bray that evening, sights Madge had never seen before, possibly because they were best seen with a companion, and at the end of the evening when the busker left her to the last train for the city and he said,
'See you next week Madge' it seemed that like the buses, Madge had not won a lone jackpot but that two had come along together for her.

The Fortune Teller

Madam Romani plied her trade in Albert Walk and had done so for many years. She was not really a Roma as she liked people to think, but was in fact a native of Bray, but a romantic and foreign sounding name was necessary in this business, who was going to cross the palm of a Maggie Mooney with money to be told a fortune she reckoned?

Trade used to be better years ago but now people were sceptical and didn't believe in fortune telling any more but still she set up her stall every summer and if the weather held up there was usually a crowd in the resort most weekends, and at least a few were, if nothing else and they didn't really believe in it, up for a laugh and came to her to have their fortunes told.

It was the August weekend, nearing the end of the season and up to this the season had been slow, the weather was not good and with the advent of foreign holidays, well it seemed to Maggie that it may be time to consider a new career. A number of premises in the Walk had already closed due to the decrease in the number of people walking through it and who had outgrown Bray and were taking cheap foreign sun holidays now.

Bank Holiday Sunday was a washout, it rained all day, which kept the punters off the streets. Jesus she thought, if she could really see the future she would have stayed home today instead of wasting her time sitting in a cold draughty room in a fancy dress costume waiting for customers who never came.

As she stood and looked out the window onto the deserted lane way that was Albert Walk the gulls were making a racket overhead and Gerry Sullivan the busker was singing to himself in the lane and she, despite her own predicament, felt sorry for him and felt like tossing him a few bob to go and get in out of the rain and have a burger and a pint somewhere. As she stood taking pity on Gerry she suddenly heard footsteps on the stairs. That's strange she thought, I didn't see anyone come in. She took the few steps back to her place behind her table on which she had for effect and to impress the punters, a crystal ball, a few candles and other bits of 'Magic Items' she had bought years ago in Hector Greys in Dublin, and they were old enough now to look authentic.

She adjusted her costume making sure her own clothes were hidden, she still had to be convincing and the sight of a modern garment showing under her Roma costume was not conducive to convincing anyone that she was a real fortune teller, a real Roma. She was good at what she did and realized that first impressions were important.

As the footsteps got nearer she cleared her throat and prepared to put on the false accent she used to fool her clients. She sat quiet still awaiting the person, whoever it was, to come into the room. She always left the door open when she was alone in case someone wanted a fortune told.

As she waited in anticipation for whoever it was to show themselves she heard a voice. She listened carefully and realized whoever it was was speaking in a foreign language. In her own false accent she called out
'Come in. Come in please, Madam Romani is available to tell your fortune'

Then to her surprise a lady dressed in Roma clothing entered the room and began speaking to her in a foreign language. Maggie Mooney was speechless and as the lady continued speaking in a language she could not understand she reverted to her own accent and said,
'Please, I cannot understand a word you are saying, can you not speak in English?'
The lady smiled at her and said, 'Yes I can speak in English, but I am surprised that a Roma cannot speak or understand her own language'

Maggie was speechless and did not know how to respond or what to say to the lady who had by now sat on the chair opposite her and was smiling benignly at her. Then when she had gained some measure of composure she asked, 'Who are you and what do you want'

'I am the Roma fortune teller that you are impersonating, I am Madam Romani' the lady replied and only then did Maggie realize that they were dressed in identical clothing, right down to the colour of the nail polish they were wearing and the rings on their fingers

'You have culturally misappropriated my identity, you have assumed my identity for financial gain' the lady said and Maggie had no idea what she was talking about, cultural misappropriation was totally meaningless to Maggie, she had no notion what it meant, she only dressed like she did to make a living.

'I'm just trying to make a living' she replied because she truly did not know what else to say.

'There are other ways to make a living besides misappropriating someone's identity' the lady said and Maggie still did not know what that was.

'What if I was to dress as you and present myself as something I was not, would you not be offended by that?'

Maggie did not reply because she still did not know what was happening and therefore what to say.

'I'm sorry if I offended you' Maggie then said because she did understand the meaning of the word offend, and would never knowingly offend anyone.

'Thank you, that at least is good to know' the lady said and then asked Maggie,

'Can you tell fortunes, can you tell the future?'

'No' Maggie replied, 'of course not, nobody can do that it's all a game and the punters know that, it's all for fun'

'Would you like to be able to see the future?' the lady then asked, 'would you like to be able to see what's to come?'

'Nobody can do that' Maggie again replied.

'I can' the lady said, 'and I can let you see the future too, but not so as you make money from it. The future is not a commodity to be bought and sold, the future belongs to everyone'

Maggie remained silent and considered what the lady had said and then asked,
'Who are you?'

'I am the person you can become. I am the you of the future, and of the past, because the future is just a continuation of the past that has progressed through the present and left there a blueprint for what's needed to be done so as to carry on the time continuum, just as I am doing now'

Maggie thought about what the lady had said and struggled to understand it but as she began to think about it she looked at the crystal ball on the table and she could see visions, visions of an older version of herself and she was telling fortunes and the people, the punters were it seemed thanking her profusely and she began to understood what the lady meant.

'Is that me?' Maggie asked the lady and indicated the vision in the crystal ball.

'It can be, but only if you have the confidence to be the person you really are and not misrepresent yourself as something you are not'

'You have given me a lot to think about, whoever you are' Maggie said and stood and looked out the window with her back to the lady and Gerry the busker was still there and he was eating a burger and a bag of chips, and when he saw her looking at him he gave her a thumbs up and continued eating his burger.

When Maggie turned back to face the lady she was gone and the room was empty. The lady was gone but she had not heard her go nor had she heard footsteps on the stairs as she left.

When she herself left soon after, Gerry was still singing his songs to the rain and the gulls and as she passed him she said goodnight and he replied and said,
'Thanks for the few quid Maggie I had something to eat and I'll get a few pints on my way home, you're a generous lady'

On Bank Holiday Monday, which was a lovely sunny day Maggie Mooney turned up in Albert Walk in her own clothes and did not change into her Romany costume. She took down the Madam Romani sign and put up a sign which simply said 'Maggie Mooney Fortune Teller, All Fortunes told Free'

Jonathan and Mabel's Protestant Passion

Jonathan Layfield was a Protestant in a city full of
Catholics and for that reason he found it a bit difficult to find
romance. He was not a particularly religious person but he
did value his heritage and all things being equal would have
had a preference for a Protestant romantic partner, but where
to find one was his problem. He worked in a soap factory in
the city as a general factory hand and his Protestant work
ethic and his enthusiasm to blend in with the predominately
Catholic work force made it a near certainty that he would
progress fast in his job. He even went as far as joining in the
recitation of the Rosary every Friday afternoon in the factory
canteen before finishing for the weekend such was his
determination to blend in and make progress in his job.

As recompense for this betrayal of his faith he went to
church twice every Sunday, in the morning for Service and
later for Evensong. It was in church that he met Mabel Coates.
She was the daughter of good friends of his parents and if the
truth be told it was both sets of parents who were more
enthusiastic about them getting together than they were
themselves, but Mabel was attractive in a Protestant sort of
way, which differed from Catholic attractiveness in that
Protestants tended to dress to hide their physical attributes
whereas Catholic girls tended to emphasise theirs and
Jonathan tended to prefer the Catholic way. But to please his
parents he went along with their attempts to bring himself
and Mabel together. How he would ever have met a girl, a
good Protestant girl other than in church in this city he did not
know so he and Mabel began going for walks together after
morning service and he began to enjoy her company.

Still there were some girls in the factory that he fancied and would have liked to go out with but they were all Catholics and although he flirted with them and was attracted to one or two of them in a physical sort of way he never actually got around to asking them out. He did not personally discriminate on a religious basis where he got his romance from but he knew he would be disappointing his parents if that had happened so he continued to see Mabel as there was it seemed nowhere else to meet Protestant girls other than in the church and Mabel was, well she was fun to be with and had a mischievous sense of humour, not at all like a typical Protestant girl and she did tend to dress more like a Catholic than most Protestant girls of her age and that pleased Jonathan too.

Before meeting Mabel he had often passed the time by going to Bray in the summer on his own because he knew that quite a few North of Ireland people went there for holidays and many of those holidaymakers were like him of the Protestant Faith, so besides the church Bray was a place he thought he might meet someone of his own faith and he listened carefully for a northern or Scottish accent. In fact he actually had met a Protestant girl one time there but she was an Episcopalian and he was Church of Ireland and when he got to know her a bit he found that she was more dogmatic in her views on religion than even the Catholics were and her morals were of such a high standard that nothing beyond hand holding was permitted.

He knew it would not work out between them and so that potential romance went nowhere. Although he had no real success in the romance department there he was fond of Bray and especially of Albert Walk, the laneway close to the station that he always walked through to get to the prom. It was full of souvenir shops and amusement arcades and such like and he often went into one of the amusement arcades to try to boost his spending power for spending on other things in Bray but he nearly always lost more money than he had intended to lose and so wished he had just kept walking or had instead stood and listened to the busker who always seemed to be there in the lane. He was pretty good and always sang what was popular at the time and he always threw a few pence into his hat. Then one day shortly after he had begun to go out with Mabel and she was beginning to---well beginning to arouse sexual feelings in him he was in Bray on his own and on the way to the prom on his walk through Albert Walk he noticed a new guest house had opened and it was recessed just a little way back from the main walkway which gave it a somewhat------secretive and mysterious kind of look. He could imagine Humphrey Bogart or some such person walking out of it with his lover. It was the kind of place you would see at the pictures. It was he believed the kind of place you would choose to have a rendezvous with a lover in, and for some reason he began to think of Mabel and how he would like to spend the night there with her and make love to her there but he thought if he said that to Mabel she would think he was a pervert or some such thing as good living Protestant girls never had thoughts of sex or pleasures of the flesh, that was a Catholic thing, or so he believed. At first such thoughts embarrassed him and he tried to put them out of his mind, saying to himself 'Sure what would a good clean living Protestant girl like Mabel think of me if I suggested anything like that, spending the night together in guest house before we were married!' and he passed the house and went on his way.

The following week after service, and because it was so fine and sunny he asked Mabel if she would like to skip Evensong and go somewhere, to Bray he suggested. Mabel to his surprise and delight was agreeable and so they decided to skip Evensong this week and go to the beach instead. And so after Service ended they said their goodbyes to their family and friends, but did not say where they were going or that they would not be at Evensong. Both their families, conscious of the scarcity of eligible young Protestant boys and girls in their community were so glad and happy for them that they had found each other and were they hoped well on their way to playing their part in increasing the Protestant population of the city, but not of course until after they were married.

They headed straight to Amiens Street Station after Service and got a packed train to Bray. It was hot on the train and they were crammed together like sardines and somehow Jonathan managed to find himself with Mabel sitting on his lap because the compartment was so packed, this was something that had never happened before. They had never been in such close physical proximity since they had met. They were only a matter of months going out together and had only up to then held hands with a slight, a very slight peck on the cheek and a chaste hug when they were parting and Jonathan being a clean living Protestant man was reluctant just yet to become more physical in the relationship in case it would offend Mabel. After all there were rules about such things and they had to be observed but now through no fault of his own he found himself with Mabel sitting on his lap and him with his arms around her holding her close to him.

As the train bounced along Jonathan found himself being thrust against Mabel and the vibrations this caused made him feel very uncomfortable and not being in a position to do anything about it he became embarrassed in case he would cause Mabel to be offended. As the train chugged along and his embarrassment became more intense he tried to manoeuvre Mabel on his lap so that she would not-----well not feel the reason for his embarrassment. But to his surprise every time he tried to adjust his position Mabel moved back into a position that meant she was sitting precisely where he did not want her to sit and she seemed not to mind the discomfort she must have felt. As he once more tried to adjust position Mabel looked at him smiled and said,
'It's alright Jonathan, it's only natural'

He was amazed to hear her say that and seeing as she it seemed had no objection to his aroused state he relaxed and enjoyed the experience and even on one occasion as the train came to a somewhat jerky stop in moving his hands to stop her falling forward found himself cupping her breasts in his hands with her hands covering his and holding them tight against her bosom for longer than was necessary.

Eventually they reached Bray and by then there was a little more room in the train as quite a few passengers had got off at Dun Laoghaire, Dalkey and Killiney and Jonathan and Mabel were sitting side by side now and Mabel was resting her head on Jonathan's shoulder. The earlier excitement had abated somewhat but Jonathan's head was buzzing with sensual pleasure at how Mabel had behaved when she was sitting on his lap and how she had held his hands against her breast when he tried to stop her falling forward when the train came to a jerky stop. He was full of anticipation of how things would go with them later when they were alone and found some secluded spot to whisper sweet nothings into each other's ear.

As they got off the train holding hands Jonathan led Mabel towards Albert Walk and as they passed the new guest house Jonathan said jokingly to Mabel,
'If we miss the last train we can stay there for the night'
'Do you think we'll miss the last train?' Mabel asked and smiled.
'I haven't got a time table, do you?' Jonathan replied and squeezed Mabel's hand and she reached her head up and kissed him on the lips. Things were definitely hotting up between them.

They spent the day in the glorious sunshine on the beach where Mabel took off her top to sunbath and Jonathan got to put sun cream on her back. He had seen and touched more of Mabel in the last few hours than he had ever seen or touched of any girl in his life, and to make it all the better she was a good clean living Protestant girl.

Later they had a meal of fish and chips in a cafe and as evening descended they went and had an alcoholic beverage in the Esplanade Hotel. This was a first for both of them, because as traditional Protestant's they did not drink alcohol but the freedom and the romantic and erotic vibes they were generating in each other encouraged them to lose some of their strict Protestant inhibitions in anticipation for what each of them knew was to come.

They spent the rest of the evening in the funfair and then when darkness had descended and they were walking dreamily along the prom they heard the sound of the whistle of the train and Jonathan looked at his watch and said,
'Gosh, it looks like we've missed the train'
'Oh Jonathan I can't sleep out in the open, you'll have to get me a bed for the night' Mabel said and smiled at Jonathan

'Yes that would never do, a gentleman should always protect the virtue of a lady. I know just the place where we can get shelter for the night' he replied and looked into Mabel's eyes and kissed her on the lips, and not just a peck on the lips but a kiss that held the promise of even more passion to come.

And so holding hands and smiling broadly they headed towards Albert Walk and the new guest house Jonathan had seen. They represented themselves as a married couple and although the proprietor knew differently he allowed them in and showed them to a room with a double bed and said as he closed the door on them,
'I hope this room is to your satisfaction and you sleep well and we see you both back here again in the future'

No sooner was the door closed than Jonathan took Mabel in his arms and kissed her passionately on the lips and she responded in kind. Then as they disengaged from the embrace and looked into each other's eyes he, with shaking hands undid the buttons of her top as she made no effort to stop him, and breathing heavily Mabel stripped him of his shirt and trousers.
When they were both naked they stood looking at each other and giggled, each of them seeing for the first time the naked form of a man and woman and Jonathan smiling broadly as he reached out for Mabel said, 'We'll burn in hell for this'
'Then let's make it worth burning for'
Mabel replied and she threw herself into Jonathan's arms and they fell onto the bed and in a frenzy of excitement and passion began attempting to increase the Protestant population of Ireland before the fires of hell consumed them.

Dead Man Talking

Vinny Murphy woke up dead on Christmas morning. He knew he was dead because he could not smell the incinerated piece of ham he had left boiling in the pot on the cooker on Christmas Eve before he went out and then forgot about when he came back from the pub where he had spent the day celebrating the festive season. He lived alone over an amusement arcade in Albert Walk in Bray since his marriage broke up ten years ago.

His former wife Joan lived with the new rich man in her life in an apartment, one of the new luxury ones that had recently sprung up in the town near the old Tudor style town hall on the top of Main Street.

He sometimes seen them out socialising on a Saturday or Sunday night in one or other of the bars on the prom and whether it was his imagination or just sour grapes but Joan he thought never looked as happy as he remembered her being when she was with him. By Jasus he often thought when he saw them, despite your mans money she doesn't look very happy since she left me, he must not be up to her high sexual expectations, well she didn't appreciate it when she had it.

Still what was done was done and that was all water down the Dargle now so it was and he was living his life as a very happy and contented forty five year old man in the prime of life, just awaiting his next love conquest, which he had to admit to himself, and only to himself, was a long time in coming. Still despite everything he was happy ------until now. Now he was a less than happy and contented corpse.

He loved to have a ham sandwich on fresh crusty bread with loads of Colman's mustard after his few pints on Christmas Eve. He had been doing it for years and it now qualified as being as much a ritual as Christmas itself.

'Fuck it' he exclaimed when he realized what had happened, that he was dead, 'And I didn't even get to have a last ham sandwich! And that was one thing I always loved about Christmas, the ham sandwich on Christmas Eve. Oh I know you could have a ham sandwich any day of the week but there was something special about the Christmas Eve one, it was as if the pig that was supplying the meat for it knew he was to be eaten on Christmas Eve and had gone on a special diet of spicy slops so that he would have that Christmassy taste about him. Still if I'm dead I'm dead, and that can't be helped now but if I come back by Jasus I'll be more careful the next time'

And then looking around the room and seeing the state of untidiness it was in he said,

'Jesus whoever finds me will think I was a dirty bastard by the state of this place' and then casting his eyes to the corpse in the bed said, 'Oh Christ did I change me underpants yesterday' and he attempted to lift the cover that was tucked up around the chin of the body in the bed.

'Fuck this I can't lift the bed cover' he exclaimed as his fingers seemed to pass through the cloth.

'What will people think if my underpants are soiled, and they might be because I remember having an almighty shit in the pub and the state I was in I may not have cleaned meself right. Oh well that can't be helped now either, if I have a shitty arse someone else will have to wipe it'

Then he began to laugh,

'That's one compensation for being dead I suppose you get someone to wipe your arse for you'

He then went and looked out the window onto Albert Walk. It was covered in a brilliant white four inches of fluffy snow.

The lane looked so Christmassy.

'Ah Jasus' he exclaimed 'For the first time since I was a kid it's snowing on Christmas Day and I'll miss it. I wonder can I leave this room or do I have to wait here till someone comes for me, to take me to Paradise------or the other place. And speaking of someone coming for me, where is everyone? I thought there would choirs singing and load's of people waiting for me to welcome me to---well to wherever I was going, but there's nobody here but me and-----that other me on the bed. Jesus death can be very lonely so it can. Can I sit down while I'm waiting I wonder' he said and gingerly attempted to sit in the armchair near the fireplace.

'You can do whatever it was your custom to do provided it does not cause a change in the destiny of others' boomed through whatever passed now for his mind and he fell into the chair with the shock of the vibration he felt.

'Jasus this is going to take some getting used to' he said and into his mind came the thought with what he thought was a hint of sarcasm,

'You have eternity to get used to it'

As he sat in the chair he could see the snow continuing to fall in the lane and he knew there would be very few out and about today and therefore his body was destined to remain undiscovered for today at least. He then though of the thought intrusion that he had heard in his mind, 'You can do whatever it was your custom to do'

Well it was his custom to go visiting on Christmas Day so maybe that's what he would do today. It would be just another normal Christmas Day-----except he would be dead when he went visiting.

He raised himself from the chair discovering as he did so that he only had to think of rising and he was, without any effort on his part, in a standing position. He thought of the lane and he no sooner had the thought than he was standing in the snow covered Albert Walk. 'Jesus' he laughed, 'Talk about beam me up Scotty, this is like being an actor in Star Trek'

As he moved his feet he looked down and he was making no impression on the freshly laid snow and as he 'walked' towards the train station a young couple were laughing as they crossed his path and he called out to them 'Happy Christmas' but they ignored his greeting and passed before him as if they did not see him.

He continued on his way and headed for the sandy part of the beach near the harbour where he knew there would be hardy swimmers partaking of the charity Christmas Day swim. He mingled amongst them recognising some of his friends and as he wished them a happy Christmas they ignored him too.

After watching the swimmers for a while and discovering that he could walk on the water, as he did as he walked alongside some of his friends who were swimming, he decided to be on his way and headed for the house of his best friend John Mulvey who lived with his wife and family in a house just off the Main Street of the town. As he entered the house through the closed door he felt a bit like an intruder because although he did not intend to do any harm he did not like them not knowing he was there.

'What time is it Kay?' he heard John ask of his wife.

'Oh he'll be here any minute now so he will it's half ten' she replied.

'Hide that bottle of whiskey or he won't leave till its empty' she then said.

'Ah Kay sure we are the only friends he has on a Christmas Day, if he didn't come here sure where would he go?'

'Well he could start with his former wife. I know she still has feelings for him and that clown she's with now gives her a terrible time, did you ever see her looking so unhappy. At least when she was with him she had a smile on her face most of the time for some reason'

Vinny listened to this with a sense of sadness and amusement.

'Did I really drink all their whiskey' he wondered and tried to think of the many Christmases past he had visited but somehow could never remember leaving after his visit.

And Joan, had she really got feelings for him after all this time and the smile on her face-----well he knew why that was there. He hung around for a while as John and Kay waited for their visitor and then when after a time and when John had gone and looked down the road on two occasions to see if he was coming they decided he was not coming this year and John poured himself a whiskey and said,

'To you Vinny pal wherever you are, Happy Christmas'

He smiled to himself and said

'Happy Christmas John and Kay enjoy your whiskey, seems like you'll have it all to yourself this year'

He then headed to the apartment Joan shared with the man who could not put a smile on her face and when he got there, although it was after midday and it was Christmas Day the blinds were still down and there was not a Christmas light or decoration to be seen.

He looked into the living room and Joan's partner, he did not know his name he then realized, was spread over the table fast asleep with an empty whiskey bottle and glass beside him and the room was littered with other bottles, beer, wine, and spirits all over the floor. He went to the bedroom and Joan was sitting up with a glass of brandy in her hand wearing a negligee with one strap off her shoulder exposing her breast and she was crying.

Although they were now separated ten years his heart went out to her when he remembered how it used to be with them, and he thought of what Kay had said, that she still had feelings for him and he realized as he looked at her with tears rolling down her face that he had feelings for her.

He attempted to put his arm around her shoulder but it seemed to go through her and he just sighed, 'Jesus Joan' he said, 'Maybe we were too hasty in separating, we had a good thing going but neither of us realized it at the time. Me thinking because I pleased you so much I could spread it around and be a regular Casanova to the women of Bray. Some Casanova I turned out to be, living alone in a room over a cheap amusement arcade with not a woman in sight, except for the sad widows who frequent the slots in the place below me, and you sitting crying in bed in a sexy negligee on Christmas Day because your rich partner is inadequate in the sex stakes.

Well we've got to live with the consequences of our actions I suppose, you for the rest of your life and me-----well I've got eternity to rue my mistakes'

With that he decided to go home and keep his corpse company until someone realized he had not been seen in his 'usual haunts' He smiled at the term which was so appropriate now he realized, and said to himself 'no pun intended' and laughed out loud until a tear ran down his cheek. He left the apartment and went home to see who would have the pleasure of finding him in the room in Albert Walk. He slowly made his way back and as he passed the few people out and about, possibly visiting friends and relatives, he said Happy Christmas to each of them without getting a reply from anyone. When he reached Albert Walk Gerry Sullivan was busking on the corner and as he casually passed him he said, 'Happy Christmas Gerry'

'Happy Christmas Vinny' Gerry replied and smiled and winked at him as he passed.

The First Great Bray Air Show

Paddy Sharkey was fourteen when the war broke out, he was twenty now as it was coming to an end and he was a LDF cadet leader and stationed at the anti- aircraft battery near Killiney not far from his home in Bray.

There was a war going on all over Europe but in Ireland there was 'An Emergency' At least that's what Dev and his soldiers of destiny called it and Paddy and a few of his friends from Bray had signed up to do there bit for the cause.

He lived in Albert Walk a laneway that ran from near the train station to Albert Avenue. Nothing much happened in Albert Walk since the war started, even The Roxy cinema was often closed, so Paddy thought that by signing up with the LDF he'd get a bit of excitement into his life.

Night after night Paddy and his compatriots met at the corner of Albert Walk and as Gerry Sullivan the busker serenaded them for their act of bravery in stepping forward to defend the Nation they cycled from their meeting place to the hillside in Killiney and manned the guns on the green sloping grass overlooking the sea near Killiney Village.

In case any of the pilots in the planes they were waiting to blow out of the sky were confused about where they were the word EIRE was helpfully marked out on the hillside so they'd know where not to drop their bombs, couldn't have the pilots wasting their bombs on a neutral country.

Paddy had been a member of the crew that manned the guns at Killiney for the past two years, since he was eighteen, and in all that time he had not seen so much as a hostile seagull flapping its wings in anger, much less an angry German Luftwaffe plane.
It was all so boring.

Word was doing the rounds that the war was almost over, Hitler had it seemed run out of ammunition and men to do his bidding and any day now a white swastika flag was expected to be unfurled by the Germans and then they could pack up the unused guns and ammunition on the hillside and go home to a less dangerous form of boredom and Dev could declare the Emergency over.

Then one night in early May as Paddy and his friend Matt Redmond were casually gazing out to sea and talking about the time they had wasted on the Killiney hillside and how they could better have spent it with their girl friends in one of the cafes or The Roxy in Albert Walk, a slight buzzing sound interrupted their conversation and they both raised their LDF issued binoculars and scanned the horizon.
'There it is!' Yelled Paddy and pointed to a small white light to their right as it made its way up the Irish Sea from the south.
'Who's is it?' Matt yelled.
'Who the fuck cares, it's not ours that's for sure so it's invading our airspace. Man the battery, man the battery, enemy planes approaching' Paddy yelled and the other four cadets scrambled to their posts and manned the two gun battery.
The light was still a bit away in the distance and one of the others asked, 'What do we do now, we don't know who's it is'
'Blow the fuckers out of the sky and ask questions afterwards, remember the North Strand' Paddy yelled.

As the plane came into range they could see it was definitely a German plane, a BV 138 Flying Clog by the shape of it, they had been fully briefed on the names and shape of the German planes, and it was approaching the long stretch of water between Bray and Killiney apparently going to attempt to land, it was a so called flying boat and landing on water was possible.

As it was descending Paddy turned his anti- aircraft gun in a southerly direction and with the barrel loaded and the direction set on the incoming plane yelled Fire! For the first time since he had been stationed on the hill a shot had been fired in anger and the incoming plane quickly began to rise from the line of descent it had been on and rose into the night sky.

The plane had been noticed in Bray too and a crowd had assembled on the seafront as the BV 138 made its way up the coast and a loud cheer went up as the sound of the anti - aircraft fire was heard and the biplane rose sharply into the air. It headed out to sea and then turned back in the direction of Bray once more and to Paddy and the lads on the hill at Killiney it seemed like that it was going to attempt to land again.

They waited until it was again within range and the two guns were now trained on the incoming plane. As it headed straight for the prom in Bray Paddy again yelled fire and his compatriots unleashed the fire power of the two anti-aircraft guns at their disposal and this time the incoming plane was hit as it headed directly for the prom in Bray and with an almighty explosion it lit up the night sky and it fragmented into pieces as it fell into the sea.

There was pandemonium on the seafront in Bray as the by now big crowd of onlookers that had gathered scrambled into the water in case there was any survivors.

While all the pandemonium was going on in Bray Paddy and his comrades were celebrating having struck a blow for Ireland and saved the country from a possible German invasion.

As far as they were concerned the war was over now and Gerry would not dare to invade Ireland again, now that they knew the strength of the gun power awaiting them, and if they did they'd be ready with more of the same.

With the war being declared over from the hillside in Killiney the lads decided to go back to Bray and celebrate their victory over the Germans and so they shut up shop on the hill and cycled back to Bray to get a pint before the pubs closed, though they thought they would stay open a bit later tonight to celebrate Ireland having just won a war she was neutral in.

The pubs did indeed stay open late and Paddy had a sore head the next morning having had to consume a multitude of pints that were bought for him and the lads because of their heroism in defeating the Hun who had dared to invade Ireland.

The next morning, the first day of the end of the Second World War, or to give it its rightful name 'The Emergency' crowds descended on Bray to see the wreckage of the German Air Force that had been destroyed by being blown from the sky over Bray by a battery of guns of the LDF. Even the Irish Air Corps came out to see the wreckage and provided great entertainment for the crowds as their planes flew in formation in the sky above the scene of the destruction of the German Air Force as the crowds below cheered them to the rafters.

There was a carnival atmosphere in Bray all day and Paddy and his small company of heroes were feted everywhere as the boys who had shot down Hitler's plane as he tried to escape his fate. Yes, the local grapevine soon had it that The Fuhrer himself had been on the plane. He had been trying to land in Ireland, so the word was, to persuade de Valera to give him the lend of the Irish Army to finish the war in return for a promise that when he defeated England he would personally hand back the six counties to Dev.

When that news got out Paddy and the lads soon lost their hero status and soon became known as the boys who had cost Ireland the chance to be A Nation Once Again and Paddy was not much pleased with that.

And how did the knowledge that Hitler had been on the plane become known? Sure hadn't someone of them that had plunged into the sea to rescue any survivors of the shooting found a piece of human flesh, an upper lip with a small black moustache attached to it and sure what German could that have belonged to but Hitler!

He that found it then sold it to the owner of one of the amusement arcades in Albert Walk and sure to this day people are paying good money to see the lip of the Fuhrer that was saved from the wreckage of the plane that was shot down over Bray the night of the First Great Bray Air Show.

Midnight At The Roxy

The Roxy wasn't in Albert Walk at all, well the entrance wasn't, it was on Albert Avenue but Joe Carroll who lived on Albert Walk always said it was, because he said, when you walked in the door of the cinema you left Albert Avenue and were then in Albert Walk. Therefore he always maintained as the main part of the cinema was in fact in Albert Walk, The Roxy cinema was in Albert Walk.

Anyway there was going to be a midnight matinee on Friday night in aid of some charity or something and he was looking forward to it. He was not often out at midnight, mostly because there was nothing open at midnight, or indeed after midnight as he would be on Friday because the film to be shown, 'Casablanca' was well over an hour long and that would take you to near two o'clock in the morning.

Joe was eighteen years of age and he was in love with Lily Kelly, who was seventeen, but he had never told her so. He had told no one. In fact he had hardly even spoken to Lily, just the odd bashful 'Hello' when he saw her on the street or sometimes when he saw her in The Roxy. He was a big film fan and he went to The Roxy at least twice a week and he knew Lily was too because of the number of times he saw her there, and like him she always seemed to be alone. Hopefully Friday night would change all that he thought.

He knew Lily worked as a sales assistant in a fashionable clothes shop on the main street of the town because he worked in the butchers shop two doors away. That's how he first noticed her. She was beautiful he thought and he could imagine her trying on the dresses that were on the mannequins in the shop window to show the customers how they looked on a real live person, but he could not imagine them looking as lovely as he was sure they looked on her. She was tall for a girl, almost as tall as he was and he was almost six feet tall, she had long dark hair and she was slim, but not skinny, she had all the things a girl should have and she wore mostly them new mini skirt's that showed off her shapely legs that he admired so much. And the fact that she was a film fan was an extra added attraction for Joe.

When the midnight matinee was announced he saw it as the opportunity he wanted to speak to Lily. He knew she most probably would like to go to the show but being a young girl and seeing as she always went to the cinema on her own he thought that maybe she would like a companion for such a late night event. He did not know where she lived but seeing as she worked in Bray and went to the cinema in Bray he reckoned that she must live somewhere local and-------well he was assuming a lot but that's what lovelorn young men sometimes do.

Anyway on the Monday before the Friday the midnight matinee was scheduled the tickets went on sale and Joe borrowed his work colleague Paddy Clark's bike and cycled down to the cinema during his lunch hour and purchased two tickets for Friday night's performance.

'You've just got the last two tickets Joe, the show's a sell out, a good job you came down now or you would be going to bed early on Friday' Mary Butler the cashier said as she handed Joe the tickets.

'Who are you bringing?' She asked knowing that Joe usually went to the Roxy on his own,
.'What lucky lady is going to melt into your arms at the end of such a romantic film?' She asked as Joe blushed in embarrassment.

On the way back to work Joe saw Lily Kelly rushing down Albert Avenue in the direction of the Roxy and he almost ran into a car coming in the opposite direction who beeped his horn at him as he looked after her and he wondered if she was in fact on her way to do what he had just done. If so she was going to be disappointed he thought and smiled to himself.

The next day in work a number of customers expressed disappointment at not being able to get a ticket for the midnight matinee and this news kept the smile on Joe's face, tickets were it seemed at a premium.

Wednesday was Joe's day off. One of the disadvantages of the job was he had to work most Saturday's because that was a busy day in the butchery business and he had Wednesday off in lieu. He slept late on Wednesday morning and after a late breakfast he rambled down to the beach and played the slots for a while and then bought himself an ice cream cone and sat eating it on the wall at Fontenoy Terrace near Bray Head. As he was day dreaming about Lily and how things might work out on Friday night and not paying attention to the passing parade of people heading to or from the Head he heard a voice say,
'Hello, you haven't been stood up I hope?'

He disengaged from his reverie and to his absolute surprise it seemed like his day dreaming had assumed mortal form. Lily Kelly in all her loveliness was standing before him with a white Poodle on a leash like one of them film stars and she was smiling at him.

In his surprise he jumped from the wall and in so doing his cone fell out of his hand to be promptly consumed by Lily's Poodle. 'Well that's his after dinner treat taken care of' Lilly smiled and Joe felt mortified for being so clumsy as he was still in a state of shock that she had actually spoken to him and this caused him to drop his cone.

'No, no ----it's ---I have Wednesday off because I work Saturday. The shop does be busy on Saturday' he replied and his voice then seemed to cease working as he stood looking at Lily and her dog and seemed incapable of saying anymore. Lily after waiting for Joe to continue the conversation, which it seemed he was not going to do then said,

'Well it was nice meeting you, sorry about your cone' and began to walk away.

'Say something! say something! say something you big idiot' A voice screamed in his head and as he watched as Lily and her dog walked towards the Bray Head Hotel he ran after her and without any preamble spurted out,
'Are you going to the midnight matinee on Friday night?'

Lily stopped and turned and replied,
'No, afraid not, couldn't get a ticket they were all sold out. Are you going? '

'Yea, yea I am'

'You must have got there early, I went on Monday at lunch hour and they had just sold the last two tickets'

'Yea I know----I mean I saw you on Monday, I had------I mean I saw you running down Albert Avenue'

'Was that you on a bike who nearly crashed into a car heading back towards town?'

Joe smiled embarrassingly and said 'Yea yea that was me'

'What were you looking at that you almost ran into a car? Lily asked an increasingly embarrassed Joe.

'I don't know, just day dreaming I suppose' he replied.

'Anyway enjoy the show on Friday' Lily said and began walking away.

'Would you like to------would you like to----go?' Joe asked as Lily continued walking away.

She stopped and turned towards Joe and asked, 'Go? Go where?'

She was not making it easy Joe thought.

'To ----To--- To the midnight matinee?'

'Yes I would. But I don't have a ticket remember'

'I have' Joe replied.

'I know but I don't'

'Jesus' Joe thought, 'women, why do they have to be so difficult'

'I, I, I got you one' Joe stammered and his face went red.

'You did?'

'Yea well I ----I'

'Why did you get me a ticket?'

Exasperated and frustrated by Lily's questioning and lack of understanding at his attempts to ask her to the show Joe just ignored her question and blurted out,

'Would you like to come with me, to the midnight matinee on Friday?' and waited for Lily's reply with baited breath.

'Was it you who bought the last two tickets on Monday?'

'Yes'

Lily then smiled and looking at Joe in a somewhat embarrassed way said,

'Well I have to be honest with you. I already knew that. Mary Butler told me she had just sold the last two tickets to you and since I knew that you always went to the cinema on your own and Mary said you got all embarrassed when she asked who was the young lady you were bringing and------ I just had to know too who that young lady was'

'What! -----' Joe exclaimed 'You mean you knew all along I had bought a ticket for you and you---- you--------'

'I did not know you had bought it for me' Lily retorted, 'Well not for sure, well you're not the only one who----I've been attracted to-------Oh---I took today off because I knew that you did not work on Wednesday's and I ------I followed you and thought maybe you were going to meet----meet the girl you were going to bring to the midnight matinee------ and I wanted to see her, to see who she was'

Joe smiled at Lily and now that he knew there was something between them he got all cocky and sure of himself and said,   'And so tell us this now, did I? Did I meet that girl? Are you going to come to The Roxy with me on Friday night then or what?'

Lily smiled shyly and replied,

'Yes, yes I'll go to the Roxy with you, no point in wasting a valuable ticket now is there?'

And so on Friday night Joe met Lily and they took their place in the queue that snacked around from Albert Avenue and into Albert Walk to await the opening of the Roxy as a busker played and sang 'As Time Goes By'

The Pub Outing

Joe and Marie Sweeney were big fish in a small pond. They lived in a small artisan type house in the midst of a neighbourhood of tenement buildings. Joe was small and dapper and smoked cigars, more for effect than that he enjoyed them, and always wore a suit in an area where most men wore trousers, a white shirt and a cardigan six days a week and 'The Suit' was only worn on Sundays as it spent the rest of the week in the Pawn, and Marie was glamorous compared to the rest of the women in the neighbourhood and went regularly to the beauty parlour on Berkley Road to keep herself that way. Joe was a car salesman in the LSE motor company on Frederick Street which would have been the equivalent of a computer technician or such like at some future time and earned good money in the age of the rapid growth of the mighty automobile which allowed him to be dapper and Marie to be glamorous.

In a way they were the envy of their neighbours who looked on them as the aristocrats of the neighbourhood. They had the electricity installed in the house and a radiogram with a collection of American records and on warm summer Sundays Joe would throw open the parlour window and a crowd would gather outside to hear Michael O'Heiher's voice paint word pictures of the big match of the day from Croke Park.

They even had a motor car, a shining black Morris Minor, registration number ZL 8785 that was Joe's pride and joy and they seemed to want for nothing in a time when most people had nothing.

They should have been happy beyond words and to the world they inhabited they were, but when they closed their door and discarded their street persona they were sad. In the silence of their pristine home they could hear the multitude of children playing street games outside and they knew that despite all they had by way of material goods they were lacking in one thing, they had no children.

They were now in their forties and had been married for over twenty years and were still in love with each other but that love would have been so much more complete if they had children, or even one child.

Every Friday and Saturday night Joe and Marie put on their happy face and joined their neighbours in the local pub for a few pints and a chat which kept them in touch with their less well off neighbours and invariably at some point during the night the conversation turned to the children and the antics they were getting up to and it was at that point that Joe could see the sadness and longing in Marie's eyes and he wondered why they could not have children too.

They had been to the doctors and despite getting a clean bill of health the child they longed for just did not materialise. That one piece of their happy ever after jigsaw was missing. They had everything, a nice home, money, each other, and they even went on holidays every year. No one, but no one in the street ever went on holidays. That kind of thing was unheard of. A one day outing to the seaside organised by the local pub was the nearest thing to a holiday anyone ever went on but Joe and Marie never went on those outings, until now that is.

They were just back from Galway where they had spent the week sheltering from the rain in The Great Southern Hotel and Joe still had a week to kill before he returned to work and the weather had turned glorious, the rain clouds were gone and the sky was bright blue and the sun had reappeared and everyone was out in their summer finery and the pub outing was on that weekend.

Joe and Marie felt they had had no holiday with all the rain they had endured in the west and actually envied those going on the outing.

'Do you think we should see if there are any ticket's left for the outing?' Marie asked Joe.

'The outing? Sure we never go on that' Joe replied dismissively.

'Maybe we should go this year, after all we've had no holiday this year with that awful weather we got in Galway and the weather is lovely now, it would be great to spend a few hours sunbathing by the sea'

'Ah I don't know, sure we'd have to sit in a bus for hours so we would and I'm not used to that. I like to do the driving when I'm travelling'

'No we wouldn't, sure they're only going to Bray this year. They went to Ballybunion last year and everyone was giving out about the short amount of time they got to spend there before they had to come home so they decided to go somewhere nearer this year'

'And they're going to Bray? Sure that's only down the road. I'd go there in little more than a half an hour in the car so I would. Why are they going there?'

'I told you, they want to go somewhere near so they'll have more time to spend there'

'More time to spend in the pubs if you ask me, sure they might as well just stay here and-------'

Joe then looked at Marie and said,
'Do you know what love maybe we will go, but not in a bus. If they're only going to Bray sure we can drive down and meet them there'
'Ah Joe sure the whole purpose of the outing is so as we can all be together and mingle and have a bit of a laugh'
'Well that's the only way I'll go, there'll be no buses for me, Jesus Marie sure I can't remember the last time I was on a bus'

Despite his affability Joe could be a bit of a snob when it came to his status in the neighbourhood, as I've said big fish in a small pond. They discussed it at length and in the end Marie got her way and Joe went down to the pub and meekly asked Mick Dempsey the bar man if there were a few spare tickets left. There was and Joe handed over the fifteen shillings for two tickets that included tea, sandwiches and soup in The International Hotel and a return trip to Bray, on a private coach Mick the barman reminded Joe.

There was amazement in the pub when word got around that the local royalty were honouring them with their presence on the trip and that Joe and Marie were actually going to travel on a bus with the common herd and someone suggested that the two seats in the front of the bus be reserved for them and marked with two paper crowns that they could wear for the day. That got a laugh but was not carried through.

The great day came and Buglers opened early so that the revelers could have a drink before departing for Bray and so they would get into the holiday mood for their big day out. The weather was continuing to hold up and everyone was in their summer finery including Joe and Marie, Joe even sporting a straw hat and chewing on a cigar that Mr. Churchill himself would be proud of and Marie all dollied out in a new summer dress she had bought in The Silk Mills in Dorset Street that drew gasps of admiration from the other women.

The bus that had been hired from CIE arrived all decked out in coloured ribbons and balloons which went some way to disguising the unwashed drab green colour of the vehicle and the travellers were eventually persuaded to get aboard, some it seemed would have been just as happy to have spent the day in Buglers.

When it was established that all who should have been aboard were aboard, including Joe and Marie, not in the front seats as had been suggested by someone as a joke but in the body of the bus, the door was closed and the sandwiches that someone had brought was passed around. Joe when he got on made his way up the aisle and sat in a seat in the middle of the bus, he had heard a whisper and was not going to sit anywhere near the front. The bus eventually pulled away and the revelers were given a rousing send off by those who for whatever reason were not going on the outing to Bray.

No sooner had they left the street than the singing started and it continued all the way to The Silver Tassie on the Bray road where it was insisted the bus should stop for a toilet break, even though they were within pissing distance of their destination at that point.

'Jesus Marie' Joe said when they were stopped 'I had no idea it would have been like this, me ears are killing me from all the noise, do these people ever stop singing?'
'Ah sure they're enjoying themselves so they are, can you not be happy for them. They seldom get out like this'

'They're going to Bray for God sake, not Blackpool, do they not understand that?'

Eventually after over an hour in the Silver Tassie the bus driver had to threaten that he was leaving in five minutes whether anyone was on the bus or not before they continued their journey.

Five more minutes or so later the bus pulled up outside Bray train station and the now well inebriated passengers got off, some stumbling off and nearly doing themselves an injury which would have necessitated them spending the day in Louglinstown Hospital instead of Bray. They stood at the station in a trance waiting for someone to tell them what to do next or where to go and the bus driver stood on the step of the bus and looked at his watch and said, 'Ladies and Gentlemen, it's now half past one and I'll be back here with the bus at nine o'clock sharp to take you back to Dublin. You have seven and a half hours to enjoy yourselves in Bray so make the most of it. And remember nine o' clock and I'll not wait a minute longer'

And with that he got behind the wheel and drove the bus away still displaying the bunting and balloons as the already groggy passengers stood and watched while a busker played on the corner of a laneway across from the station and some of the more inebriated passengers joined him in singing while dropping a few pennies in his hat.

'What will we do now?' Joe asked Marie as the others dispersed in all directions.

'There's a nice little tea room over there on the corner' she replied 'will we go and have a cup of tea first before we do anything?'

So they walked the short distance from the station and entered the tea room on Albert Walk. The room was packed and it looked as if all the tables were occupied as Joe and Marie stood at the door and looked to see if there was a table free.

'You can sit here if you like' an elderly man with a thick white beard who was occupying a table on his own at the window said to them. Joe looked at Marie and she smiled to acknowledge the gesture and they sat at the man's table.

'Thank you so much' Marie said to the man, 'we won't be disturbing you for long, we just wanted a cup of tea before we began our day in Bray'

'On a visit then are you?'

'Yes' Joe replied, 'on a day trip from Dublin'

'Well you've got good weather for your trip'

'Yes it's lovely so it is' Marie replied.

They sat with the man and Joe ordered tea and scones and asked the man if he would like to join them but he declined as he had already ordered.

'What's Dublin like these days? A good place to bring up children is it? The man then asked.

Marie and Joe exchanged an awkward smile and Joe then said, 'We wouldn't know anything about that I'm afraid, we don't have any children'

'Oh' the man exclaimed, 'You look like a pair that was made to be parents. I bet you'd make great parents so I do, if you don't mind me saying so'

'Well I'm afraid that we have never had the opportunity to-------' Joe replied and he looked at Marie and she had her head cast down and he knew what she was thinking.

'Well sure you never know the Lord works in mysterious ways and it's not too late yet' the man said and reached over and touched Marie's hand. They had their tea and scones in near silence then, only the occasional comment about the weather and how they were looking forward to their day out and then Joe said,

'We better be on our way or the day will be over and we will not have seen Bray at all' and he reached out and took Marie's hand.

'Yes that would be a pity not to see Bray' the man said 'Bray is such a magical place, especially on a day like this. Do you know they say that when you can see the coast of Wales from the top of Bray Head, as you can today, you can make a wish and it will come true. Can you believe that?'

'Do you live in Bray?' Joe asked

'Among other places' the man replied 'I get around'

Joe did not know how to respond to that answer so he just smiled at the man and said

'Well it was nice meeting you and thanks for allowing us to sit with you. Come on Marie, we had better go' and he stood waiting for Marie to join him but she looked at the man who was looking at her with such compassion in his eyes that she was compelled to ask, 'Who are you?'

'My name is Attam, though that is unimportant, I am but a messenger'

'That's a strange name. It's not Irish is it?' Marie asked.

'It is what you seek'

'I don't understand' she replied.

Attam smiled at her and said,

'On a day such as this I am here to give true meaning to my name and to fulfil your fondest wish'

'How do you know what my fondest wish is?'

'I know, and it shall be done according to the grace of God. Before the summer is over, before the first winds of winter disturb the leaves on the trees your fondest wish shall be granted with a gift from God'

Joe and Marie began to feel a bit uneasy at the way the conversation was going and bid the man goodbye then and left the tea room and stood in a trance outside the door somewhat traumatised by what the strange man had said and then Joe said to Marie,

'Wait here for a minute I'm going back to ask that man just exactly what he meant by ----' and he went back into the tea rooms and there was no sign of the man they had just left and he asked the lady behind the counter if there was a toilet, thinking he may have gone there but he was informed that there was no toilet on the premises and no back exit either, and no she did not remember a customer as described by Joe ever being in the tea rooms that day.

When Joe informed Marie of his conversation with the lady behind the counter in the tea room she was confused and they spent a somewhat puzzled day walking around Bray thinking of what the man had said and each hoping against hope that he might be right. They even made the climb up Bray Head, and yes the coast of Wales was just about visible on the horizon far out at sea and under the cross on top of the head they made a wish.

When they got home later that night Joe decided to do a bit of detective work on the unusual name the man had given and he discovered from his copy of 'The Encyclopaedia Britannica' that Attam according to ancient legend meant 'A GIFT FROM GOD' and furthermore before Christmas came around Marie's fondest wish had indeed come true as she discovered she was pregnant. When the child was born in the spring it was a boy and they called the child Albert on account of the strange encounter they had in the little tea room in Albert Walk on the day of the pub outing.

The Eternal Busker

Gerry Sullivan had played The Theatre Royal back in the day, he was a star then and there was talk of London and Broadway beckoning to him. But because of circumstances outside of his control, now instead of playing The Albert Hall he was busking in Albert Walk. But he was not disappointed because he realized that he was fulfilling his destiny, he was standing where a long line of his kind had stood and sung to the passing crowds. Albert Walk is where he was meant to be on the stage of life and always had been.

Sometimes as he played his guitar and sang his songs someone would recognise him and with a nudge to their companion point out the busker with the hat on the ground to collect the few coins tossed his way, and indicate that he used to be 'The Great Gerry Sullivan' It was true, he had actually heard someone say that and he had felt like running after them and pointing out that he still was 'The Great Gerry Sullivan' and always would be 'The Great Gerry Sullivan' for as long as there was an Albert Walk there would be a 'Great Gerry Sullivan' to play there.

More fool they for not recognising that greatness.

He was, it seemed to the passersby, always in Albert Walk, morning noon and night, rain or shine and the strange thing was nobody ever saw him arrive or leave his pitch, it was as if he was a permanent fixture there, a part of the furniture as was the saying.

To each new generation that passed through the lane he was known as the busker in the lane. But he did of course leave his post from time to time, or more precisely from age to age as time went by and he reappeared to each new generation of day trippers as another version of the 'Great Gerry Sullivan' the man who had not realized his potential and ended up busking in a lane in Bray and each new generation had their own story to tell of the fall of 'The Great Gerry Sullivan' and each story was true because he was The Eternal Busker who chronicled each page of history with his songs.

To the Victorians he was someone who had performed for Queen Victoria and her Consort Albert and The Royal Family and had a fabulous future ahead of him but had somehow managed to get on the wrong side of a powerful personage and had paid the price for it and was now reduced to performing on the streets of Bray for his transgressions.

To another generation he was the singer who sang the songs of the workers who defied William Martin Murphy and the dastardly bosses and for that he had his potential greatness snatched from his grasp and like the defeated workers lost the chance to realize his full potential.

To yet another generation he was the busker who sang rebel songs as the bullets flew in O'Connell Street and paid the price of his rebelliousness by having his career shot down in its prime just as the rebels were executed in theirs.

As Collins and Dev fought over the treaty he was content to remain neutral and sing his songs of the New Ireland that was coming. And for that deed he fell between two stools and was not allowed on either of them when hostilities ended.

But he still sang when the new state was formed and a long dreamed of Independence was won and then again when The Four Courts went up in flames and the dreams of a nation were put on hold.

He never stopped singing his songs of hope for better times even as brother fought brother and the nation shed tears of blood.

When war in Europe was raging and in Ireland an Emergency was declared he stood his ground in Albert Walk and sang his songs of peace.

He later picked up the sounds of Negro jazz emanating from the clubs of Harlem and in his way made it fit his repertoire. Side by side with the sean nos songs of Heany and Harte he blended the melodies to fit his style.

He was inspired by the Hippy generation, by Dylan, Seeger and Joan Baez and the season of love that came and went and had promised so much but yielded so little except for the songs he sang so well.

And then when John, Paul, George and Ringo appeared he took up his guitar and followed their beat.

Whatever was in fashion, whatever was the style that was the music the busker played that brought the land alive. Blues, Jazz, and, Rock and Roll, Country and Soul too, sure even Wee Daniel got a hearing in The Walk when the busker was in town.

The seasons passed the times they changed and still he sang his songs until the day he looked up and no one was around. The coins had stopped filling his hat and the shutters had come down, most of the shops in the lane were gone and there were no day trippers to confound. But old habits die hard and still he sang his songs for no reward because he realized that if he stopped the music, he would be no more too. The music was his life blood and so he would sing till the day he died, and beyond that if he could.

So if some day you happen to walk down the old lane and it's deserted but you somehow hear a song being sung though no one's around, that's the echo of the music bequeathed to the nation by 'The Great Gerry Sullivan' The Eternal Busker who's spirit still abounds and sings his songs and plays his guitar and awaits the return of the crowds to Albert Walk to once more sing his songs for them.

Albert Walk 2060

The Greater Dublin and Urban Area Redevelopment worker attached the stone extractor and crusher around the old stone marker which read 'Albert Walk 1886' and was about to pull it out of the ground at the corner of the old deserted laneway that was just across from the Water Artery Rapid Transport station that was being extended to accommodate the increased number of passengers that used the WART transport service.

The WART had replaced the DART in the 2050s and got you from Bray to central Dublin in twenty minutes and was powered by powerful turbines that used the sea water from the Irish Sea to rapidly propel the carriages along the water filled trench that replaced the rail tracks. Adrian Connety the foreman on the job seeing what was about to happen shouted to the workman,

'Stop Gary, let's have a look at that marker before you destroy it' and he went to the old stone marker and ran his hand over the stone letting, his fingers tracing out the date 1886.

'Just imagine' he said to the worker standing by to do his job 'that stone has stood in that same spot for 174 years telling people they were in Albert Walk and in a moment it will be gone and we will have erased the knowledge that there ever was an Albert Walk in Bray'

'Yea well that's progress I suppose, sure who remembers the old football ground that used to be across the road there where the Mosque is now? Or the old Victorian bandstand that was dismantled on the prom to make way for the new turbo powered chairlift to the new Bray Head Hotel on top of the mountain, or where the Aquarium used to be when it was decided that keeping fish in tanks was cruel? All of them gone in the name of progress. And anyway it was only an old unused laneway that will be put to better use when the new station is complete' Gary Lane the workman replied.

'Yea I suppose so but what I wonder would those that used the walk down the years think if they knew it was going to be no more, obliterated like so much more of old Bray?'

'Adrian I have a job to do, do you mind if I do it?' Gary asked as Adrian stood up and looked at the marker and said, 'Yea well as you say that's progress. But Gary will you do me a favour? When you pull that stone out of the ground will you not destroy it? I mean don't pulverize it like all the other old stones. I know a place where it will be safe for another 174 years'

'You're stone mad Adrian, but if that's what you want, sure I'll save it for you'
'Thanks Gary. I think there's a bit of history in that old stone that it would be a pity to destroy, you know the saying if stones could talk'

If stones could talk indeed and if that stone in particular could talk what tales it could tell. 174 years ago when it was laid the very idea of a WART system of transportation was science fiction, if indeed there had been such a genre back then.

But it had been the means of telling countless generations of Bray inhabitants as well as millions of day trippers where they were and it had seen so many changes taking place in the town. It had witnessed the lane and the people who passed through it since Victorian times and seen it when it was a thriving place of commerce and entertainment and seen its demise when people stopped walking through it and the places of business like the tea rooms, amusement arcades and the souvenir shops began to put up the shutters and close. But soon it would be no more as would the laneway that countless thousands of day trippers had walked through on the way to the prom and seafront in Bray.

As Adrian watched Gary activated his machine and the stone, like a tooth being extracted slowly parted company from the earth that had been its resting place for the past 174 years.

'So what do you want me to do with it now Adrian?' Gary asked as the marker dangled in the air on the arm of the extractor mechanism.

'Just put it down gently over there' Adrian said and pointed to the old ruined building behind them.

'It will be safe there until I can arrange to get it taken away'

Gary did as requested and swung the mechanical arm with the dangling stone across the already broken exterior wall of the old building and laid it safely on the floor and Adrian went about his business assured that his stone was safe as Gary then began the work of dismantling the heavy stones that had formed a border of some sort all the way down the laneway on the left hand side.

Later that day Adrian came back to see that his stone was safe for the night and when he looked over the wall of the ruined building to his astonishment the floor had collapsed and the stone marker had fallen into the basement.

'Dear God that stone must have been heavier than I thought, it collapsed the whole floor'

He peered into the darkness of the basement but he could see nothing as it was completely dark and dusk was falling as well so he decided to wait till morning when there would be better light and get a better idea of the damage and the state of his stone.

Next morning he met Gary and told him what had happened and asked him to get a light rigged up so that he could see where his stone was.

'I had no idea there was a basement in that building' Gary said when Adrian told him what had happened.

'According to the old plans of the layout of the place it used to be an old amusement arcade back in the dim distant past when Bray was a popular holiday resort, when peopled actually holidayed in Ireland and there was no cheap space exploration holidays on offer'

'Well there is a basement and my stone has fallen into it so can you rig up a light and a ladder so that I can get down there and see where my stone is?'

'Right so I'll see to it straight away Adrian'

When Gary had organised the light and ladder Adrian went down into the basement and started searching for his stone marker. He was amazed to find a collection of old rusting gambling machines of the kind used back in the mid to late twentieth century and a few pieces of old furniture, chairs and a table and a few pieces of crockery as if someone had lived there. He rummaged around the basement and as his light cut through the darkness he seen what appeared to be a bundle of clothes or some such thing and he went to the bundle and as he looked closely at it he realized that it was an old tattered sleeping bag and it appeared to be covering some class of object.

He very cautiously lifted the covering with a piece of wood he found on the flood and to his absolute shock and horror he found a skeleton of what appeared to be a human being. He scarpered out of the basement as fast as he could and raised the alarm. Soon all work on the site came to a halt as the police authorities descended on the lane and began an investigation into who the skeleton could possibly be and how long it had been there.   In the course of the examination of the skeleton it was discovered it was clasping in its hand an old rusted pendant or locket of some sort but because of the length of time it had been in the basement it was corroded and could not be opened or separated to see if it could throw any light on who the skeleton might be. After an investigation it was discovered that no foul play had occurred in the death of whoever the skeleton was, there were no marks or indication of violence, whoever it was had died of natural causes and had lain undiscovered in the old building for almost a hundred years.

A funeral service was arranged as it was deemed that the man, it was a man, must have been, as most people were back then, a Christian. The pendant or locket was left in the hand of the skeleton when it was buried as whoever it was was clasping it so tightly that it must have meant something special to him.

As the work that was going on would mark the end of Albert Walk as an address in Bray and as Adrian, a native of Bray, was anxious to keep the name alive he asked permission to use the old stone marker that had been responsible for discovering the skeleton be used as a headstone for whoever the skeleton had been. As the stone marker would have been destroyed in normal circumstances this was agreed to and so it was decided to add the date 2060 to the marker as a reminder that the last time a human had resided in Albert Walk was 2060, even if that human was a dead one.

On the morning of the funeral of the unknown skeleton a huge crowd of Bray inhabitants turned out to say goodbye to whoever the person had been, and in a way to say goodbye to Albert Walk.

In using the old stone marker as a headstone for the skeleton they were acknowledging the fact that Albert Walk had existed just as whoever the skeleton had been had existed too and would always be remembered as being a part of Bray.

All those present at the funeral witnessed a most unusual occurrence. As the cortege left the vicinity of the WART station just across from Albert Walk, it had been decided that is where the funeral would depart from, a busker, something that had not been seen or heard of in Bray for generations appeared on the corner of the now sealed off Albert Walk and as the skeleton was taken to his final resting place he walked ahead of the cortege singing a song that had been popular many, many years previous, 'Time To Say Goodbye'

Made in the USA
Columbia, SC
13 June 2022